classic

an it girl novel

CREATED BY

CECILY VON ZIEGESAR

poppy

LITTLE, BROWN AND COMPANY
New York   Boston

Poppy

Hachette Book Group
237 Park Avenue, New York, NY 10017
For more of your favorite series, go to www.pickapoppy.com

First Edition: June 2010

Poppy is an imprint of Little, Brown and Company
The Poppy name and logo are trademarks of Hachette Book Group, Inc.

alloyentertainment
Produced by Alloy Entertainment
151 West 26th Street, New York, NY 10001

Cover design by Andrea C. Uva
Cover photograph by Roger Moenks
Canine cover model: Zoë Belle Conescu

ISBN: 978-0-316-07395-0
10 9 8 7 6 5 4 3 2 1
CWO
Printed in the United States of America

it girl novels created by Cecily von Ziegesar:

The It Girl
Notorious
Reckless
Unforgettable
Lucky
Tempted
Infamous
Adored
Devious
Classic

If you like **the it girl**, you may also enjoy:

The **Poseur** series by Rachel Maude
The **Secrets of My Hollywood Life** series by Jen Calonita
Betwixt by Tara Bray Smith
Haters by Alisa Valdes-Rodriguez
The Daughters series by Joanna Philbin

The heart was made to be broken.

—Oscar Wilde

A WAVERLY OWL IS ALWAYS FILLED WITH A SENSE OF JOY UPON RETURNING TO WAVERLY.

The cold February wind whipped across the snow-covered Waverly Academy fields, cutting right through Easy Walsh's thick Patagonia jacket. He pulled his Hugo Boss scarf tighter around his neck. It was much colder in upstate New York than it had been in West Virginia, where he'd spent the past few months of his junior year suffering through military school. He was going to have to get used to a real Yankee winter all over again, and it had been hard enough the first time, when he was a freshman. As he followed the salted and scraped pathway across the quad toward Richards, the boys' dorm he'd never expected to live in again, he decided he'd much rather freeze his ass off than drop and give some blowhard twenty push-ups.

Easy threw the butt of his cigarette under his boot and blew out the last of the smoke, watching the cloud form in the frigid night air. The ivy and brick Waverly campus—more brick than ivy this time of year—seemed unusually quiet all around him. Tonight was the last night before classes started for spring term, and historically that was a time of widespread revelry for Waverly's hard-partying student body. Instead the night seemed hushed—from the dark sky alive with stars above him to the empty stretch of fields and lawns still covered with ice and snow. The uncharacteristic quiet was probably due to the harsh punishments everyone had been given after the big party in the new dean's house a month ago. Particularly strict probation, he'd heard, and he knew from personal experience that meant the Waverly Academy version of being grounded: stricter rules about coed visitation, early lights-out, and the generally clueless teachers paying much closer attention to the social lives of Waverly Owls than usual. In short, it sucked.

Easy's eyes scanned the lit windows of the dorms that ringed the quad. Owls were probably stuck in their rooms going stir-crazy while they waited for classes to start and probation to be lifted.

It had been some party.

Easy had sneaked back onto campus that night to visit his horse, Credo, who was stuck at the Waverly stables thanks to a transportation snafu, which Easy's stern, corporate father had naturally decided was Easy's fault. As if Mr. Walsh needed any more reasons to find his artistic, underachieving youngest son exasperating. Easy was pretty sure his father had been annoyed with him since the day he'd been born.

Easy had planned to spend a little time with his horse and

then disappear again. He *hadn't* planned to walk into a totally illegal party at the brand-new dean's house, much less to save the dean's daughter, Isla, from breaking her neck. But she'd been falling, so he'd caught her. What else could he do? When Dean Dresden had revoked his expulsion, readmitting him to Waverly as a personal thank-you for saving Isla's life, Easy had been thrilled. He'd gone directly to see Credo, as originally planned, and had pretended not to think about his ex-girlfriend Callie Vernon at all—until she'd walked into the stables in the middle of the night and found him there.

He'd been forced to finally admit to himself that Callie was the real reason he'd hopped a bus to Rhinecliff, New York, and Waverly Academy when he was supposed to be headed back to military school a few days early. Despite the fact that Callie had lost the promise ring he'd given her and had mercilessly dumped him on top of the Empire State Building over Thanksgiving, and despite the fact that, when he'd seen her at the party at Dean Dresden's house, she'd been holding hands with Brandon Buchanan, Callie was still on his mind.

Callie. It was always about Callie, one way or another, and it was always complicated.

He hoisted his battered North Face duffel high on his shoulder and took the steps of Richards two at a time. He shouldered his way through the heavy outer doors and then ran up the familiar stairs inside to the room he'd shared with Alan St. Girard before his expulsion. Home, sweet Waverly home.

He pushed the door open and looked inside, not really surprised to see that Alan had done very little with his unexpected single besides throw his dirty laundry on Easy's empty bed. Alan was the most laid-back guy Easy knew—a condition Alan carefully maintained by smoking huge quantities of the pot his liberal, hippie professor parents grew on their New Hampshire farm. The faintest scent of pot smoke and incense clung to the hardwood floors and emanated in bursts from the ancient heating pipe that rattled and clanked in the corner. Alan had been in the room recently, though there was no sign of him now.

Knowing Alan, he was probably sacked out in the common room, sleeping through another Godfather marathon or watching *Family Guy* on DVD.

Easy thought about taking the time to throw Alan's laundry back on his side of the room so he could unpack his stuff, but he just couldn't deal with it. He felt restless, as if there were an electric current running through him, keeping him off-balance. He threw his duffel in the general direction of his bed and ran his fingers through his almost-black hair. He was still surprised to find it so short. His hair had been the first thing to go when he'd arrived at military school, but for some reason he still expected to feel the longer, curlier hair he'd had the last time he'd lived in this room. The truth was, he still didn't quite recognize the guy he saw when he looked in the mirror these days.

Easy blew out a deep breath. He felt as if the walls of his old, familiar dorm room were closing in on him. And there was only one way he knew to make that feeling go away. Only one thing he could think of that would help him make sense to himself.

He turned around, walked out the door, and headed back

down the stairs, nodding absently to a couple of freshman boys whom he passed on the way. He heard them whisper his name as he went, but he didn't turn back around. He forgot them the moment he pushed open the outside door and felt the winter slap him in the face again.

The night outside was still so cold, it made the denim of his beat-up old Levi's feel stiff against his legs, but a big, bright moon was rising, peeking over the bare branches of the trees and reflecting off the dark waters of the Hudson River as it quietly wound its way past the Waverly campus. Easy didn't have to think too hard about where he was going. He let his body lead the way, moving him across the campus like it had its own GPS and autopilot, until he found himself back where he always seemed to end up: beneath Callie's window.

Her window was lit up from within and cracked just slightly to let the typical Waverly radiator-heat overkill out into the night. Or maybe because she'd been smoking a cigarette earlier.

He kicked around in the ice and snow at his feet until he scraped out a handful of pebbles. He jiggled them in his palm for a second, calming himself down. Then he stepped back and took aim.

Callie Vernon lay across her bed in Dumbarton 303 with her MacBook propped open on her stomach, twirling a strand of her strawberry blond hair around her index finger. The laptop felt like a hot-water bottle against her flat stomach, and her plaid flannel Juicy pajama bottoms felt equally cozy. They were her favorite—so good at keeping out the winter chill on long, cold nights like this one.

She read Brandon's latest e-mail for the second time, smiling. He'd gotten in the habit of e-mailing her every night before he went to sleep, counting down the days until their Jan Plan probation period ended. Or the *prohibition period*, as some people were calling it. Whatever you called it, it had been a loooong month of way too much studying and far too little partying.

Callie was actually looking forward to classes starting the following day, which was unusual. Mostly, she was tired of all the enforced single-sex bonding that was all she'd had by way of entertainment throughout the cold, boring month of January.

She slid the hot laptop off her stomach and stared across the room, with its dark wood floor and high ceilings. But she barely saw any of it—not the riot of clothes (mostly hers) tossed across the extra bed, which was shoved against the wall from back when 303 had been a triple, or even her roommate Jenny Humphrey's bright bohemian-print bedspread and cheerful pink and yellow pillows. All she could think about was what had happened after the party at the dean's house. That single, amazing kiss she'd shared with Easy Walsh out in the stables— the one that, even a month later, made her pulse pound and her stomach twist.

Callie swung her legs over the edge of her bed and let her bare feet slide against the cool wood beneath her, absently admiring her pale peach pedicure. Easy had disappeared after that kiss. She hadn't told Brandon about kissing Easy—at first because she'd been holding it close to her heart like some kind of lucky charm, but then because she had known that it would hurt Brandon's feelings. And the more time she spent with Brandon—even the supervised, practically Amish time that was all they'd had in the past month—the less she wanted to hurt him any more than she already had over the course of the past few years.

Part of her wondered if it had all been a dream—Easy appearing in the middle of the party like that, his lips against hers in the dark of the stables . . .

Callie froze when she heard the clatter of pebbles against the foggy window. Was she asleep right now? But no—a few seconds later, she heard the same noise again.

She was on her feet before she knew she meant to move, drawn to the window by the irresistible force that always seemed to pull her to him, no matter what. She couldn't see through the fog on the glass, so she wrenched the old, rattley window open and leaned out—

And there he was.

Easy.

Callie drank him in. He seemed so different, his deep blue eyes glittering in the night, his dark curls shorn short, somehow making his eyes that much more intense. Callie couldn't seem to say anything, even though she'd thought she'd saved up a thousand things to tell him if—*when*—she saw him again. She could only stare down at him. His months in military school had changed him. He didn't smile. He was bigger—more muscular—and he stood straighter. But none of that mattered;

if anything, it made her itch to discover how else he might have changed.

"I'll be right down," she whispered into the dark. He nodded.

She turned from the window in a kind of daze, her thoughts and emotions too much of a jumble to make any kind of sense. She pulled on the nearest pair of shoes she could find, an ancient pair of Uggs, and threw a fleece the color of daffodils on over her sweater. It might even have been Jenny's fleece, but for once Callie didn't care what she looked like. She didn't even glance in the mirror. She just zipped the fleece up as she left the room and hurtled down the steps toward the outside door.

She skidded around the side of the building and saw the dark figure, waiting.

He coughed. He was really there. She wasn't dreaming.

Callie made herself breathe and moved toward him.

"Hey," he said when she was close. Callie tried to search his face for a clue to what he was feeling, because with Easy she could never be sure. But it was too dark.

"Hey," she whispered. Her throat felt dry, and she realized that she was nervous. She didn't know why he'd come to find her tonight—or how long he was staying. She rocked on her heels and shoved her hands in the pockets of the fleece. "You're back."

"I'm back."

Did he still dream about her? Was he mad at her? The last time they'd seen each other had been so fast and crazy, but the time before *that* was the awful night Callie had broken up with him. She could still remember the crushed look in his blue eyes. She shivered.

"I kind of thought I made up that whole night," Callie said softly. "Kissing you in the stables."

The corners of Easy's mouth turned up, and, at once, Callie's heart felt a teensy bit lighter. It wasn't quite a smile, but he reached down and tucked a stray strand of her strawberry blond hair behind her ear, his fingers brushing her cheek in that old familiar way.

"You still with Brandon?" Easy asked quietly, still holding on to that one lock of her hair like it was the only thing anchoring them together, and he was afraid to let go.

Callie bit her lip slightly. She liked Brandon. She cared about him. But she'd never stood in the frigid cold of a winter's night looking at Brandon, thinking she might die if she didn't touch him soon. And she didn't think she ever would.

"I guess," she said. Easy's face hardened, and she hurried on. "I mean, sort of. It doesn't really mean anything. We've barely been let out of our rooms since the dean busted up that party, anyway."

"Callie." Easy's voice, and his soft sigh, sent a delicious shiver through her, and Callie didn't wait for any more clues. She reached over and slid her hands against his chest.

She couldn't tell who moved then, but she was finally in his arms, and his mouth covered hers. Callie wrapped her arms around his neck and tried to get even closer to him, kissing him again and again, until the whole world disappeared.

"I missed you," Easy murmured shyly, pulling back to look down at her, his dark blue eyes warm.

"I missed you, too," she said, happier than she ever remembered being before. It was like her whole life had been in black-and-white, and now Easy had brought in the color. Not to mention HD with surround sound. She looked up at him and smiled, reaching over to hold his cold face between her hands. "I'll make sure things are over with Brandon," she said. "I promise."

"Good." Easy nodded. And then he smiled, finally—his full, real, crooked smile, the one that showed her he was the same Easy Walsh she had been in love with forever.

2

A WAVERLY OWL NEVER DROPS HINTS WHEN
DIRECT COMMUNICATION IS REQUIRED.

"All right, everyone, it's almost curfew! This is your last chance to hand in your projects!" Mrs. Silver cried from the front of the art studio, clapping her hands together, her gray hair and apple-red Mrs. Claus cheeks looking less jolly than usual. She'd been trying to shoo the Jan Plan stragglers, who were working up to the last minute on their projects due today, out of the studio for the past half hour.

Jenny Humphrey packed her pencils and charcoals into her black canvas messenger bag and smiled at the boy who'd made her smile a lot recently: Isaac Dresden. He leaned against the desk, his green eyes focused on the drawings that Jenny had piled up in front of her. His short black curls stood up from his head in sharp contrast to the white gleam of his smile.

"I think that's it," Jenny said, straightening her pile of drawings. For her Jan Plan project, she'd decided to do an art project resembling stop-motion photography, where one object remains still while the camera captures movement all around it. Except Jenny had achieved the effect by hand, instead of with a camera. She was determined to do a good job and impress the dean with her project. Not just because she was dating his son—she bit back a giddy little sigh that always threatened to overtake her at the thought of Isaac—but because she was only a sophomore and had had to convince the dean to let her work alone in the first place. Sophomores were supposed to do group Jan Plan projects. Solo projects like the one Jenny had just completed were usually reserved for more mature and academically adventurous upperclassmen.

"Are you sure these are the ones you want?" Isaac asked. He'd helped her pick out the best drawings, and he knew how anxious she'd been about choosing the right ones. "It's a big decision. Once you turn the drawings in, there's no going back," he teased, his green eyes lighting up along with his smile. He lounged back against the desk, and her breath caught. Isaac was so incredibly cute, wearing an untucked green checked button-down shirt under a blue sweater with more than one hole thrown over battered old Abercrombie khakis. He looked like the perfect prep-school boy that he was. She was glad she'd worn her fitted emerald green J. Crew sweater, knowing it minimized her too-big chest. And the color was great against her long brown curls.

"There's nothing more I can do," Jenny said philosophically, yanking her attention away from Isaac's tempting good looks and back to her project. She ran a hand over the cover of her portfolio and tried not to second-guess the final selection of drawings that she and Isaac had just spent hours agonizing over. She squared her shoulders. "I guess Mrs. Silver and your dad will have to decide if I proved that sophomores should be allowed to do solo projects." She wrinkled her nose. "Or not."

Isaac's grin deepened. "I don't think you have to worry. It's one small step for you, but a giant leap for all Waverly sophomores. They'll love you for it."

Except when they hated her guts, which they seemed to do at the slightest provocation. Jenny walked her portfolio over to Mrs. Silver's desk and placed it carefully in the growing pile of down-to-the-wire submissions. It was hard to believe that she'd experienced so much at Waverly and still hadn't made it through an entire school year. Sometimes she almost forgot that she'd had an entirely different life in New York City at her old school, Constance Billard. A school without boys and with required uniforms! The two experiences were as different as night and day, but if Jenny had to compare them, not having to face those two factors alone tipped the scales in favor of Waverly. She fought a smile as she thought about how far she'd come. A year ago, could she ever have predicted she'd be handing in a special project and dating the dean's son?

She shrugged on her quilted orange Guess jacket and zipped it up to her chin. Isaac wrapped a gray cashmere scarf around his neck and then walked her toward the door. She couldn't help but throw a forlorn look over her shoulder toward Mrs. Silver's desk, where her project sat with all the others. She bit her lip, then forced herself to let it go. In her opinion, she'd done some of her best drawings ever, and she had to be okay with that. Her father, Rufus, always told her that no one could expect anything more than her best, and as long as she gave her best, she couldn't fail. She hoped that wasn't just his Berkeley-hippie-turned-Upper-West-Side-liberal love-in side talking.

Besides, there were more important things to consider, now that it was February. Namely, Valentine's Day.

Together, Jenny and Isaac headed out of the art building and into the cold Waverly night. His arm just grazed her shoulder as they pushed through the doors, and the sensation resonated through her body in pleasant waves.

Now that Jan Plan was over, probation was lifted, and her project was handed in, Jenny could give her relationship with Isaac her full attention. Valentine's Day was just a week away! Her head swam with visions of Isaac dancing with her at the big Valentine's Day Ball, kissing her tenderly in a sea of red and pink hearts. She and Isaac had only kissed once, just as she was about to run out the door of his father's house the night of the infamous party. It was a quick, fleeting kiss, on the back doorstep of his house. Not bad, but not exactly the most romantic moment in the world, either. Surely V-Day was an excellent time to change all that.

"Not sure I'm too psyched about classes starting tomorrow," Isaac said as they headed down the dark path that led toward the dorms. Though Isaac lived in the dean's house with his parents, he always insisted on walking Jenny to the front steps of Dumbarton.

"I'm happy probation is ending." Jenny reached into her pockets and pulled out the bright red wool gloves her mother had sent her for Christmas from Prague and worked her fingers into them.

"Sure, but I kind of liked having only one thing to concentrate on," Isaac replied. He looked at her meaningfully, and Jenny blushed. How did she get so lucky?

"Fortunately, we have something to look forward to," Jenny said, still picturing her romantic evening with Isaac. At the ball, she would wear a dress to put Cinderella to shame. She could feel the huge skirts swishing all around her as she moved, could see her curls dancing around her face, maybe even a tiara glinting atop her head. Isaac would be dressed in a tuxedo, his green eyes intent on hers. His soft lips—

"Homework?" Isaac asked dryly.

"No, silly," Jenny said, laughing. "Valentine's Day. Is it lame that I'm really excited for the ball?"

Isaac didn't say anything. Suddenly a gust of cold wind wormed its way down Jenny's back, making her shiver.

"Not that I'm into overdosing on candy or construction-paper hearts or anything," Jenny continued, a sudden attack of nerves making her talk without thinking. Had she missed something? She and Isaac had been together for more than a month now. Was she not supposed to talk about things like dances or major holidays?

"I . . . didn't realize it was so soon," Isaac said, but he sounded like he was talking to himself.

"Well, it's the sixth of February right now," Jenny pointed out. "And Valentine's Day is pretty much always on the four-teenth."

Isaac frowned. He stepped farther away from her, leaving space for another person to walk between them on the path.

"But it's okay," Jenny continued, "because there's only one thing I want for Valentine's Day. I'll give you a hint. You don't even have to spring for those chalky little 'be mine' heart candies."

They'd walked to the edge of the quad then, and Jenny was surprised when Isaac stopped. She stopped walking, too, and looked at him, confused.

"Uh, sorry," he said, clearing his throat. "I didn't realize it was so late." But he didn't quite meet her eyes. "I promised my dad we could have some family time before the term starts. I can't believe I forgot."

Jenny couldn't believe it, either—especially since they'd all been on probation for the whole month, and Isaac had just been complaining the other day that he'd had way more Dresden family time than anyone should be forced to endure.

"Okay," she said. She moved closer to him and put her hands on his hips, tilting her head back to look up at him. Isaac was much taller than her five feet nothing, which made her feel deliciously small. She smiled. "But first let me tell you what I want more than anything for Valentine's Day."

Isaac swallowed, and then he stepped back.

"I'm sorry," he said after a moment. "But, um, you know how my dad gets." He looked at Jenny and then at his feet.

"Isaac?" All of Jenny's confusion came out in her voice. Had she been too . . . forward or something? She'd never been self-conscious around Isaac. That was good, wasn't it? She'd thought so . . . until now.

"I'll, uh, see you tomorrow," Isaac said, and then he turned and took off, leaving her standing alone and completely bewildered in the dark of the empty quad.

"I just want a Valentine's Day kiss," Jenny murmured, but the cold winter wind swept her words away, and there was no one to hear.

A WAVERLY OWL NEVER SEEKS TO BE THE CENTER
OF ATTENTION; ATTENTION, ON THE OTHER HAND,
OFTEN SEEKS OUT THE OWL.

Tinsley Carmichael strode into the Waverly Academy dining hall at 8 A.M. Monday morning, more than ready for the unaccountably lame and depressing Jan Plan to be over and the new term to begin. She didn't even mind that her new Advanced Italian class met at ten in the morning on Mondays instead of the far more reasonable Tuesday afternoons of fall term. She was more than ready to embrace the new—in whatever form that might take.

She, for one, had had a shitty month.

Tinsley eyed the coffee machine and rocked back and forth in her café au lait–colored suede over-the-knee Chloé boots as she allowed a pack of awed sophomore boys to ogle her in her blue formfitting, long-sleeved Kristensen du Nord T-shirt and sleek black leggings. She smiled to herself and swept her long, almost black hair over one shoulder as she plucked an apple from the fruit display. She fixed herself a cup of mediocre but necessary coffee and wandered into the dining area.

The huge stained-glass windows stretched from floor to sky-high ceiling, giving what was actually just a cafeteria the look of a medieval cathedral. Owls were spread out at the long oak tables in their usual groups: seniors Celine Colista and Rifat Jones were huddled over their phones, as if expecting some life-altering message to appear at any moment. The repulsive scammer Drew Gately and his senior buddies were harassing Benny Cunningham and Sage Francis, two juniors Tinsley was quite certain would have nothing to do with them, upon pain of death. But then it hit her: it was Valentine's Day in less than a week, and that, historically, could mean only one thing at Waverly Academy—Perfect Match, where all the usual dating rules no longer applied.

Tinsley couldn't help grinning. Waverly tended to go a little crazy over Valentine's Day each year, but why not? Some enterprising members of the Computer Society had seized the initiative years ago and created Perfect Match. It was like a dating game for the student body: once a year everyone filled out an online personality survey, and a week later Perfect Match presented each student with his or her "perfect match" based on the results. Supposedly it was meant to break down cliques and foster Waverly spirit. Whatever. It was *fun*.

Tinsley's black Nokia vibrated in her pocket. That should be cupid in the form of her Perfect Match e-mail right now—right on schedule to liven up the new term. She set her coffee down on the nearest table and smiled vaguely at Alison Quentin, Kirin Choate, and Emily Jenkins—not that any of them were paying attention to her. They were all concentrating on their own phones.

Tinsley remembered freshman year's Perfect Match, when she'd scored a "perfect match" with none other than Bennett Styles, *the* hottest senior on the Waverly campus. Turned out he was a film buff, too. The previous year she'd deliberately filled out her survey to make sure she would get matched with Easy Walsh, just to mess with Callie's head—all in good fun, of course, not that Callie had found it too amusing at the time. And wasn't *fun* exactly what her life was sorely missing these days?

It had not been fun when adorable golden-eyed freshman Julian McCafferty had dumped her last month. The fact that she might have had it coming didn't lessen the pain, though she'd decided not to think about it anymore—a task that had not been easy, thanks to her extra-special punishment after being busted at the party at the dean's house. Everyone else had gotten strict probation, which was bad enough. But that lying Isla Dresden had blamed the entire fiasco on Tinsley when, really, it had all been *Isla's* idea. And guess who Isla's father, the dean, believed?

Which was how Tinsley found herself performing acts of community service around campus every day with Ben Quartullo, the surly middle-aged groundskeeper. Talk about not fun. This was the same man Heath Ferro had once bribed into silence with

a Cartier watch, which hadn't improved the old guy's disposi-
tion any. Tinsley's only way to pass the time was the extended
revenge fantasies she'd plotted out in her mind—because Isla
would pay for what she'd done. If she hadn't been spending all
of her time with Isla, Tinsley wouldn't have grown so far apart
from Julian, and they might still be together. The fact that Isla
had trashed her own house and blamed it on Tinsley was really
just the icing on the *things-she-needed-to-pay-for* cake.

"Who's your match, Tinsley?" Alison asked, holding her
phone to her chest, her face flushed with excitement. "I got
Parker DuBois!" Her dark almond-shaped eyes glowed with
pleasure. Parker DuBois was a gorgeous, half-French senior
with to-die-for blue eyes and golden brown hair that begged to
be tousled by willing female fingers.

"Congratulations," Tinsley said. She was building the suspense for herself by not checking her phone immediately, though
she could hear groans and squeals echo throughout the dining
hall all around her. She took a sip of her coffee as if she couldn't
be bothered with something as silly as Perfect Match, and only
when she'd made that clear did she pull out her phone.

"Rifat Jones got Teague Williams," Emily was telling the
table, her Pilates-toned body stiff with tension as she leaned forward. "Didn't you hear her scream his name like a banshee?"

"That actually makes sense," Kirin replied, frowning.
"They're both, like, athletic. But what do I have in common
with Zachary Webster?" She looked baffled. "Who *is* Zachary
Webster?"

"A freshman," Tinsley said matter-of-factly, and smirked

when Kirin groaned. Freshmen were supposed to be off-limits to upperclassmen. Obviously. If she'd followed that simple law, Tinsley wouldn't have been in a position to be dumped by one as a junior.

Tinsley flipped open her phone and scrolled to the e-mail that read *Perfect Match*. She opened it, wondering whose name it would reveal. Julian, maybe, to show him how wrong he'd been to leave her? That could be satisfying. Or—much more exciting and probably less painful—someone hot that Tinsley hadn't gotten around to really flirting with yet? Like maybe Waverly's star football player, Lance Van Brachel, who was sitting at a nearby table with a handful of his other senior buddies, exchanging high fives over someone's iPhone.

Congratulations, Tinsley Carmichael! the e-mail read. *Your perfect match is . . . Heath Ferro.*

Tinsley choked on her coffee. She almost spit it out but somehow managed to get it down without spewing.

Heath Ferro?

Really?

Tinsley scanned the dining hall until she finally located his dirty blond head in the crowd. He was lounging in a chair at a table with Lon Baruzza and Ryan Reynolds, looking as lazy and foulmouthed as ever. His air of self-confidence was complemented by his maroon Waverly blazer slung across a white Hugo Boss dress shirt. Ever since he'd had the not-so-bright idea to spend his Jan Plan camping in the icy, cold winter woods like Waverly's own Bear Grylls of *Man vs. Wild* fame—except less British and much, much dirtier—Heath had been even more obnoxious than usual.

How exactly was *Heath Ferro* her perfect match? She had pretty clearly put *smart* and *funny* in her likes column, not *horny* and *gross*. On the other hand, Heath had wanted her desperately since freshman year. She considered the possibilities. She could definitely do with being wanted desperately at the moment. Maybe this was exactly the boost she needed.

She took her time walking over to Heath's table, knowing that the slower she walked, the more attention she drew. And Tinsley was nothing if not a fan of attention.

"Hey, Ferro, guess what?" she said when she reached him, bumping her hip into the back of his chair and gazing down at him with her violet eyes. "Your dreams came true."

"Unless you're about to tell me that Jessica Alba is waiting for me in my room, preferably in a bikini, I'm thinking not," Heath replied, glancing up from the remains of his breakfast to bump fists with Ryan and Lon. His plate had leftover pancakes and the fatty remains of bacon in an Olympic-size swimming pool of maple syrup.

Tinsley gazed at her supposed "perfect match" critically. Heath might have been obnoxious, but the truth was, he was also pretty hot, with those chiseled cheekbones and green eyes. There was a reason so many otherwise smart and choosy girls had succumbed to the wiles of a guy who was *proud* of his man-whore status.

"Even better than that," she purred.

"Better than Jessica Alba?" Heath asked. He looked at her then, his dirty blond hair falling into his eyes. "Unlikely, Tinsley. Very unlikely. Alba is currently ranked number one on my To-Do list. And it's a short list."

"According to Perfect Match," Tinsley said, ignoring the typical Heath commentary, "*we* are a perfect match."

She expected one of his usual smarmy remarks—something about sexual positions, maybe, or about how many times he'd imagined this very moment while alone in his room, with only his right hand for company. She was prepared to issue the usual cutting retort—but with a little flirtatious edge, because why not? Why not play the game?

But all Heath did was nod. Like he was distracted. Or like he didn't care?

"Cool," he said.

Tinsley followed Heath's gaze and had to bite back a particularly nasty curse when she saw where—and at whom—Heath was staring.

Isla Dresden, that treacherous, two-faced bitch, was taking her sweet time walking across the dining hall, sporting a flashy gold-sequined Nanette Lepore minidress, black tights, and black Cole Haan ankle boots, her dark hair *deliberately* tousled into wildness. She looked like she should be headed out for a night of VIP room clubbing, not carrying a plastic cafeteria tray across the dining room at breakfast time.

Tinsley wanted to scratch the smug smile off Isla's pale, heart-shaped face. That might go a long way toward making her feel a little bit better about what Isla had done—and do something about the oddly deflated feeling Tinsley was currently experiencing.

"And, gentlemen, let me direct your attention to number two on the list," Heath said. He let out a low whistle. As the rest of Heath's Neanderthal friends laughed appreciatively, Tinsley could only stare with them at Isla, well aware that if she was even *on* Heath's list anymore—something that should have gone without saying—she was now ranked *below* the dean's attention-craving daughter.

She let out her breath in a huff. Was Isla *always* going to steal her thunder?

A WAVERLY OWL IS ABOVE JEALOUSY—
UNLESS PROVOKED.

Brett Messerschmidt crumbled a slightly stale blueberry muffin between her fingers and idly wished she'd gotten herself a bagel instead. A glance at her nails confirmed that her Vernis Please! Purple by Night polish was starting to chip. She looked across the table at her dark-eyed, dark-haired senior boyfriend, Sebastian Valenti. He was sprawled back against his chair, his vintage-looking John Varvatos long-sleeved T-shirt with the word BOWERY emblazoned across the front hugging his lean, muscular chest. His long legs were kicked out under the table, touching Brett's sleek black Stuart Weitzman knee-high boots while he toyed with the remains of his omelet. She only just barely kept herself from sighing with smug happiness.

Sebastian looked up as if he'd heard the sound she hadn't quite made, and his full lips curled into his usual amused smile.

"You're totally checking me out," he said, his low voice teasing.

"What?" Brett shrugged so that her bright red hair swung out from behind her ear. "Who are you, again?"

"I'm the guy you're still checking out," he said with that pure, easy confidence that sounded like a swagger. "You can't help yourself."

They'd been playing this game ever since Sebastian had admitted that while he'd dated a lot of girls before Brett, he'd never felt this way about any of them. Brett's own romantic history was a bit tangled, but she knew she'd never felt anything like this, either. Naturally, Sebastian had taken that as an opportunity to be a wiseass, which, Brett had to admit, made her feel more cherished and adored than any sweeping proclamation or intense recitation might have done.

She waved her hand dismissively, but the side of her hand caught the edge of her coffee cup. The dark, hot liquid spilled across her bright orange plastic tray, soaking her picked-over muffin.

"Great," she said, frowning at her tray. "Happy Monday morning."

"See?" Sebastian said with satisfaction. "You're so into me it makes you clumsy."

Brett stuck out her tongue at him.

"I'm pretty freaking amazing," Sebastian continued, grinning while he spread his hands out as if he were too hot to touch, "so I can't really blame you. The truth is, I actually feel sorry for you."

"I'm a little less interested in this game without coffee, Sebastian," Brett told him, narrowing her eyes at him.

Sebastian sat up and leaned across the table, bringing his full lips tantalizingly close to Brett's. His dark eyes filled with devilish glee.

"I feel so sorry for you that I'm going to get you more coffee," he said, standing up. "A splash of milk and two Splendas. Coming right up."

Brett watched him walk away, unreasonably touched that he knew how she liked her coffee—so much so that she had to reach up and feel her face to see whether she was wearing a goofy, lovesick smile. Which of course she was. Instead of embarrassing her, it just made her giggle.

The volume in the dining hall suddenly spiked, as phones everywhere beeped and rang and her Nokia vibrated loudly from the depths of her glossy maroon Burberry satchel. Brett was startled for a moment but then remembered that it was Perfect Match day—the best part of February and Valentine's Day, if you were single. It was Waverly tradition that all the Perfect Matches went to the annual Valentine's Day Ball together instead of with whomever they might happen to be dating at the time. Assuming, of course, that it wasn't the same person, which it almost never was.

A few tables away, Verena Arneval let out a whoop, then started whispering excitedly to Emmy Rosenblum, brandishing her BlackBerry. Even sad Suzanna Goldfinger, who lived next door to Brett in Dumbarton, was staring fixedly down at her flip phone at the table where she sat apart from the others, looking, well, less *droopy* than usual.

Brett gazed across the dining hall and saw Sebastian's lean

back as he bent in close toward the coffee machine. Then she glanced across the table. His phone was just sitting there, abandoned. Like he *wanted* her to check it. Her own phone was still vibrating intermittently in her bag, but she ignored it. She reached over and picked up Sebastian's phone instead.

She clicked open the Perfect Match e-mail, telling herself that she was just curious. It was funny how Perfect Match was only a survey, and yet everyone acted like the results *meant* something. Brett told herself she was simply interested in what Sebastian's results might be—on, like, a sociological level. It had nothing to do with the fact that he'd dated almost every single female member of the student body—only a *slight* exaggeration—and that Brett was a little tiny bit insecure about it.

Nothing to do with that at all.

But as Brett read the e-mail, her eyes scanning over the words until they reached a name, she felt herself freeze solid in her chair.

She had to read the name again, just to be sure she wasn't hallucinating something so vile. So . . . *unacceptable.*

Brett heard a familiar, obnoxious peal of laughter float through the air of the dining hall, and she swiveled around, knowing who she would see before her gaze found Sebastian. He was still over by the coffee machine. But this time, he was sporting a new appendage: Isla Dresden.

Sebastian leaned against the table, Isla leaning in toward him. She tipped her upper body close to his, no doubt giving Sebastian the great news that she of all people was his Perfect Match. She leaned in even closer, shaking her tousled curls back from her face, and put her hand on Seb's muscled arm. Brett reached up and fingered the ends of her short, sleek red bob.

Rather than cutting Isla off and bringing Brett—his *girlfriend*—her much-needed coffee, Sebastian was smiling. Talking. While her coffee sat in his hand, getting cold. Isla let out another rolling, riotous laugh.

Brett felt her whole body overheat, and she knew her cheeks probably matched the fire-engine red of her hair. She wouldn't be surprised if actual steam were coming out of her ears. *He was flirting.*

She knew that she should trust him—that she'd promised to trust him, and that he'd given her absolutely no reason not to.

But if Sebastian didn't want her to be jealous, then he shouldn't flirt with über-skanks right in front of her face.

A WAVERLY OWL KNOWS THAT A WELL-LAID PLAN ALMOST ALWAYS GOES AWRY.

Brandon Buchanan congratulated himself on a perfectly executed morning. His distressed brown Red Wing boots crunched into the leftover snow piled high on the sides of the shoveled and salted pathways, and the blustery February wind dropped little flakes onto his navy blue Ralph Lauren toggle coat from the trees above. He tugged his Paul Smith wool hat tighter over his ears, imagining that even from this distance, he could hear the screams and whoops and general carrying-on from the dining hall.

It was a bright but freezing Perfect Match day, and that meant full-scale Waverly madness, which Brandon had deliberately avoided by grabbing an early breakfast. This year, though, he was feeling pretty good about the whole thing. He'd slaved over his survey, carefully calibrating each response to be sure he'd be matched with Callie the way he knew in his heart he was supposed to be. He'd put down all of her likes as his, all of her dislikes as his—and he should know them, because he'd made a study of Callie Vernon for years now. Whatever happened with his Jan Plan project, he knew that his *real* work of art was his Perfect Match survey. He'd spent hours on it, and he was one hundred percent certain that he would be matched with Callie.

He veered off the main pathway and took the smaller one that led out toward the science complex, a more roundabout route toward his morning biology class. Things with Callie had been good—if a little bit distant—for the past month. It was the way he'd always imagined it would be if they got back together, and he told himself there was nothing wrong with taking things slow, easing into it. She'd been a little thrown by Easy's reappearance out of nowhere the night of the dean's party—but who wouldn't be? The guy was like some horror-movie cliché. Every time you thought he was finally gone, he'd pop right back up. This time, he was all ripped and moody from military school, which might have annoyed Brandon if he thought he had any reason to be threatened by the latest Easy Walsh resurrection.

But Easy wasn't a factor anymore. Callie was all his. Granted, they hadn't hooked up in weeks, but that was just because of the whole probation thing. They'd practically been under house arrest. If he could just kiss her again the way he was dying to do, he was sure things would be hot and amazing, like they had been before the party at the dean's house.

Brandon's phone beeped from his coat pocket, and he paused

outside the biology building. He pulled his iPhone out and glanced down at the screen, readying himself for his Perfect Match.

What. The. Fuck?

He didn't recognize the name. How was that even possible?

"Um, Brandon?"

He looked up to see a girl he'd never laid eyes on before. She was an inch or two shorter than him, with dark auburn hair twisted into uneven braids on either side of her face. She wore a Waverly blazer that hung loosely on her slim shoulders over what looked like old Gap jeans and a bright green sweater. Black-rimmed glasses completely overpowered her face. She shifted from foot to foot nervously.

"Do I know you?" Brandon asked. She blushed, and he realized how rude that sounded. "Sorry," he said, feeling like a jerk. "I just . . ." He made a half-assed kind of gesture with his hand.

"I'm Cora McSweeney," she said, and gazed expectantly at him. Her eyes were huge and brown, so large for her face that they almost reminded him of an anime character's eyes. But she was looking at him meaningfully. Was he supposed to recognize her?

"I'm sorry," he said again, waiting for her to ask him whatever she wanted to ask and then go away. He couldn't wait to text Callie and see who she'd been paired up with. Had she forgotten to turn in her survey? He couldn't think of any other explanation for their not being matched.

"I'm, um, your match," Cora said softly. She gestured toward his phone. "For Perfect Match. I'm a senior, so it's not like we were going run into each other in class or anything, so I just wanted to say hello when I saw you."

"Oh," Brandon said. Seriously? This was his match? He suddenly had a flash of sympathy for poor Stacey Fournier, with whom he'd been paired last year. She was a senior and had been insulted about being matched with a sophomore. Now, Brandon suddenly understood what she was feeling—because he couldn't help feeling a little bit insulted that *this* was his supposed "perfect match." According to whom, exactly?

"Thanks for saying hello—" he started to say.

"Well, I just wanted to—" she started at the same time.

They both broke off and laughed. Awkwardly.

"Please, um, go ahead," Brandon said. He remembered how mean Stacey Fournier had been to him a year ago. The least he could do was smile at this poor girl.

"It's okay that you have no idea who I am," she said. Her cheeks were red, but her brown eyes were direct and warm. "We don't exactly run in the same circles." Her smile was shy and a little bit lopsided.

Brandon blinked. He was surprised by how straightforward she was. In a good way. "We don't?" he asked weakly.

"Of course we don't," Cora said, her smile deepening. "It might surprise you, but there are some people at Waverly who don't hang out with Ryan Reynolds in the building his father commissioned or fly seaplanes to school like Tinsley Carmichael. Maybe not a lot." She wrinkled up her nose, holding back a laugh. "But some."

"Are you sure?" Brandon asked dryly. But he smiled.

She laughed. "That's what I've heard, anyway."

Brandon looked at her for a moment, then looked away, down the path toward his class.

Cora shook her head as if dismissing whatever she'd been about to say next and squared her shoulders. Her chin tilted up. "I'll see you tonight at the movie, I guess."

"Oh, um . . . Sure," Brandon said. Cinephiles, the film group on campus, was screening *Love Story* that night, one of the most romantic movies of all time. He'd planned to see the movie with Callie, of course. There was nothing Callie loved more than unbearably romantic movies. He couldn't wait for her to cry in his arms so he could comfort her.

"Great," Cora said, looking him directly in the eye. "I'll see you there. I might even e-mail you first." She smiled again. "Don't freak out if I do."

"Don't be silly. . . ." Brandon said, and laughed awkwardly.

Cora laughed—a real laugh—gave an awkward sort of wave, and then walked away.

It was so unfair, Brandon thought, watching her walk down the path in the crystal-bright morning sunshine. How had the computer missed his perfect compatibility with Callie, after all the work he'd put into it? It wasn't fair to him—and it certainly wasn't fair to that poor Cora girl, who had probably been hoping for a real match, someone who would get excited about going to the movie screening together or take the time to actually stop and have a conversation.

He turned to head toward his classroom but then stopped

at the bottom step of the bio building. He hadn't recognized Cora's name when he'd read it—and he certainly wouldn't have recognized *her* if he'd been asked to pick her out of a lineup. Or a yearbook. Or, really, anywhere.

But she'd certainly recognized him.

OwlNet   Instant Message Inbox

AlisonQuentin: Who's your Perfect Match?

BennyCunningham: Lon Baruzza. You?

AlisonQuentin: Parker DuBois.

BennyCunningham: Yum. Time to practice your French!

AlisonQuentin: I already know the most important phrase:
                       voulez-vous coucher avec moi?

RyanReynolds: I got Kara Whalen. Maybe if I get her drunk enough at the ball, she'll make out with a girl in front of me.

AlanStGirard: In your dreams. Did you ever stop to think why you might have been paired with a lesbian?

RyanReynolds: Ouch.

A WAVERLY OWL IS RESOLUTE IN HER DECISIONS.

Callie tugged her hooded pink Juicy robe tighter across her narrow torso and sat down on her bed with a soft sigh. Across the room, Jenny was already dressed in a pair of boot-cut black Banana Republic cords that could almost pass for Sevens and a funky, deep blue V-neck sweater. She was standing with her back to Callie, pulling her mass of brown curls into a ponytail. Callie ran her hand through her fresh-from-the-shower hair and then let it drop. She couldn't seem to get moving today, even though she had class in less than an hour and really should have been dressed already. She couldn't quite bring herself to get up and admit the day had begun—because she wanted to keep daydreaming.

Last night she'd stayed outside with Easy until they were both chilled through to the bone. Callie had come back upstairs still in a trance, before she'd happily drifted off to sleep, her mind filled with *Easy, Easy, Easy.*

"So?" Jenny turned to look at Callie, her brown eyes spark-ling. Her high ponytail swung perkily behind her. "You were going to tell me about your dreams last night. I bet I can guess what they were about," she teased.

Callie smiled slowly. "You're only half right," she said.

She'd dreamed that she was reclining on some kind of plush red velvet chaise, dressed in a fabulous Old Hollywood–esque gown, her strawberry blond hair in perfect pin curls. Easy had been stretched out beside her, his blue eyes glowing with love and his military-toned body packed into a sleek suit that the real Easy would only wear to a wedding. The dream would have been amazing enough if it had stopped there. But it hadn't. Brandon had been right there, too, on her other side. The cool, confident Brandon that Callie had fallen for all over again dur-ing Jan Plan, in a perfectly cut Burberry suit with a knowing look in his golden brown eyes.

Each one of them had held a bunch of red grapes, which they took turns feeding to Callie as she lay between them like Cleopatra. First, Easy pressed a cool, sweet grape to her lips, then Brandon teased her with the next. Callie could still practi-cally taste the fruit on her tongue.

You're a goddess, Dream Easy whispered.

You're perfect, Dream Brandon agreed.

It had practically killed Callie to wake up. No wonder she'd taken a twenty-five minute shower during which she'd com-pletely forgotten to put her Frédéric Fekkai conditioner in her hair and had only gotten out because the water ran cold.

"Wow," Jenny said softly when Callie finished describing

the dream. Callie kept the details of kissing Easy the night before to herself. Some things were private, scandalous, and all hers.

"Yeah." Callie felt her smile slip away as the truth hit her. The dream was real. Not the grape part—which was too bad, because she'd always kind of wanted to be Cleopatra—but the facts. Both Easy and Brandon were in love with her. And unlike in the dream, she couldn't have both of them at the same time.

"I never have dreams like that," Jenny complained, moving over to her desk and starting to pile up her books and notebooks. "Last night I dreamed about being late for a class and having to recite the Declaration of Independence, but in Latin. There were no grapes—and definitely no man-slaves."

Callie laughed, but her mind was racing. She pulled her knees up under her chin, watching Jenny fill her messenger bag with the materials she'd need for class. She looked over at her own bag, thrown in a heap on top of her messy desk, and sighed. Last night she'd been so sure of what to do: break up with Brandon and be with Easy. Simple. She'd never loved anyone the way she loved Easy. But wasn't that the whole problem? She and Easy hurt each other again and again and again, like they couldn't seem to help themselves. He'd even dumped her for Jenny earlier this year, and yet she'd still gone ahead and lost her virginity to him. She didn't regret it—they were like magnets, always coming together, but never for very long before they were pulled apart. And what was a magnet if it was on its own, pulling nothing?

Meanwhile, Brandon was good to her. Always. He cared about her, and he would never treat her the way Easy had treated her—or even the way she'd treated him. He was funny and sweet, and they'd spent all of last month together. Could she really throw that away, just because Easy was back? It would crush Brandon. Besides, she and Easy would probably implode the way they always did. Their relationship was way too volatile.

"What am I going to do?" she moaned, dropping her head into her hands.

Jenny stopped fussing with her school books and turned.

"You need to follow your heart," Jenny said staunchly.

Callie looked up, and absently touched the area over her heart with her hand.

"What if I want both of them?" she asked, looking from Jenny to the bright, hard winter sunlight pouring in their windows. Outside, she could see the cold ribbon of the Hudson River snaking through the winter landscape.

"I don't think they'd go for that," Jenny said with a little giggle.

Callie sighed. "Wouldn't it be easier if they would?" she asked wistfully.

Jenny frowned for a moment, leaning back against her desk, her messenger bag at her feet. Her eyes lit up suddenly. "Perfect Match!" she cried, like she was saying *ta da!*

Callie blinked. She had never been a fan of silly magazine quizzes that told you who you should be with. What did they know? She especially hadn't enjoyed last year's Perfect Match, when Tinsley had matched herself up with Easy. She'd claimed she was just teasing Callie, but Callie had always doubted the truth of that story. Tinsley just liked to cause trouble. Callie had filled out the survey this year, just because everybody did, but it wasn't like she really put stock in the results.

"I don't know what people told you, but it's just a bunch of computer geeks messing around with people for a week," Callie said gently, not wanting to shatter Jenny's little fantasy. She probably still believed in Santa Claus. "It's not like the matches really mean anything."

"You'll get paired with one of them, Brandon or Easy, on Perfect Match, and then you'll know what you're supposed to do," Jenny said firmly, putting her hands on her tiny hips. "It can't be a coincidence that the matches come out *today*, can it?"

Her petite roommate's determination forced a smile out of Callie. She scraped her wet hair back from her face. "Okay," she said, shrugging. "Sure. Perfect Match will solve all my problems."

"It will!" Jenny cried. And her own, too. She was sure of it. Last night, when she'd gotten back from her solo walk across the quad to find their room empty, she'd had nothing to distract herself from obsessing at great length over Isaac's weird behavior. Had she come on too strong? Did he not like her as much as she liked him? But then she'd remembered that the Perfect Match e-mails were coming out this morning. She'd never experienced Perfect Match before—but what wasn't to love about the idea?

Obviously, Perfect Match would pair her with Isaac, because

they were perfect for each other. And it wasn't that Jenny suddenly believed a computer program could see into people's hearts or tell the future or anything, but she figured being *proven* perfect for someone had to be worth something. It would clear up any hesitation on Isaac's part, wouldn't it? It had to.

"Maybe it really will," Callie said, warming to the idea. Her eyes looked dreamy. "Maybe I don't have to make a decision— maybe Perfect Match already knows the answer."

"Speaking of which . . ." Jenny said, waggling her eyebrows.

They both giggled and then dove for their laptops.

Callie pulled her MacBook onto her bed and opened it up, suddenly feeling jittery with anticipation. She scrolled through her e-mail until she found the one she was looking for and couldn't help grinning as she clicked on it. Maybe Jenny was right to put her faith in Perfect Match. Why not?

She blinked and read the e-mail again.

"So much for Perfect Match being a fortune-teller," she said, slapping her laptop closed and getting to her feet. "It thinks *Alan St. Girard* is my one true love." Callie shook her head. She couldn't believe she'd been paired with the biggest pothead on the Waverly campus. Seriously? "Did I fill the survey out while I was high?"

Jenny sat completely still in her hard desk chair, staring at the screen of her Dell. She blinked a few times, but the e-mail didn't change. Even though she knew it was silly, she couldn't help but feel disappointed. She didn't want Callie to see her expression, so she didn't turn around. She'd just been so sure that Isaac would be her Perfect Match. They were *meant* to be together, weren't they? She scowled at the screen of her computer, but the fact was, his name wasn't the one in her inbox.

"Let me guess," Callie said, rolling her eyes. "You got Isaac because the two of you are destined to live happily ever after."

"Actually, no," Jenny said. She turned her laptop so Callie could read the screen. Callie got up and came to peer over Jenny's shoulder. Together, they both gaped at the name.

"No way," Callie said, leaning closer.

"Yeah." Jenny slumped in her seat. "Julian McCafferty."

SageFrancis: I got Drew Gately. Um, what?

BennyCunningham: Ew.

SageFrancis: Why am I being punished?? Alison Quentin gets Parker DuBois. Rifat Jones gets Teague Williams. Brett Messerschmidt gets Isaac Dresden . . .

BennyCunningham: Tinsley Carmichael got Heath Ferro.

SageFrancis: I would happily take Heath.

BennyCunningham: I know you would. Slut.

SageFrancis: Whatever, like you can talk!

From: From: MarielPritchard@waverly.edu
To: To: [Waverly Student Body list]
Date: Date: Mon, February 9, 10:24 am
Subject: Subject: Re: Holiday Week

Dear Owls,

It is my pleasure to welcome you to the spring term.

As many of you already know (and, freshmen, please take note), February means it is time for our annual weeklong celebration of Valentine's Day, which will culminate in the Valentine's Day Ball. The ball will be held this Saturday evening in the Reynolds Atrium, which will be suitably transformed from cozy lounge space into a romantic, starlit escape for one night only. Get ready to fall in love with our beautiful campus in a whole new way!

In the meantime, I hope you are all enjoying getting to know your "Perfect Match," courtesy of the enterprising members of the Waverly Computer Society. Owls who did not receive their matches via e-mail, please contact Brian Johannsen at BrianJohannsen@waverly.edu.

We have a number of love-inspired events this week to get us all ready for our romantic Valentine's Day celebration this weekend. Please know that while these events are not mandatory, a Waverly Owl always gives back to the Waverly community by participating with enthusiasm in Academy events!

Monday night (tonight!): Come to a viewing of *Love Story* in the Cinephiles screening room. Get ready to have your heartstrings tugged by this classic film! (Please note that Owls are reminded to treat

Cinephiles screenings as movie-theater outings rather than private viewings; disruptive behavior will result in the appropriate disciplinary action.)

Tuesday afternoon: The traditional "Perfect Match" Three-Legged Race! Come to the Field House with your Perfect Match and your competitive spirit. Races begin at 3 p.m.; conflicting sports team practices will be rescheduled accordingly.

Wednesday evening: Listen to some of the most beautiful words ever written. The Drama Club is sponsoring this year's Love Poetry Reading. Bring your favorite love poem and an open heart to Maxwell at 6:30 p.m.; original poems accepted. (Please note that original poems cannot, because of time constraints, exceed one page in length.)

Thursday evening: The Dining Hall is going red! From borscht soup to red velvet cupcakes, enjoy all your favorite "red foods," brought to you *with love* by your friendly Food Services Staff.

Saturday night: The Annual Valentine's Day Ball begins at 7:30. Party attire is required. Please attend with your Perfect Match. This is your opportunity to step outside your everyday life here at Waverly, and fall in love with a whole new aspect of the Waverly experience. Rise to the challenge, Owls!

All week: As per hallowed Waverly tradition, "owl hearts" have been hidden in various locations all over campus. The Owl who collects the most hearts will be presented with the much-coveted crystal "Sweet Heart" at the ball. And then the winner will present the Sweet Heart to his or her True Waverly Love before they dance to this year's first

OwlNet

Email Inbox

dance. Who will the lucky recipient be? Could it be you? Come to the ball and see!

The Annual Waverly Valentine's Day Ball Slideshow is open for your submissions! Please send your favorite photos of "Love at Waverly" to Deanna Sebring. What is Love at Waverly to you? Is it your friends, your sweetheart, or is it Waverly itself? Share your pictures with all your fellow Owls—the slideshow will be shown during the ball. (Please note that Owls are expected to exercise discretion in the selection of photographs.)

Happy Valentine's Day!

MP

HeathFerro: Yo, who'd you get? Don't tell me it's Callie. I'll puke.

EasyWalsh: . . . um . . . Are you already drunk?

HeathFerro: Perfect Match, bro. True love and V-Day. I'm stocking up on the Jack. Consider me flasked and dangerous.

EasyWalsh I'm not in this year.

HeathFerro:: Dude. You fill out a survey and get hooked up with a hot chick for the week. It's like Craigslist.

EasyWalsh: Yeah, I know, but I never filled out the survey. I wasn't here.

HeathFerro: I wonder who Callie got matched with?

HeathFerro: EZ?

A WAVERLY OWL IS ALWAYS PREPARED TO MAKE LEMONADE FROM LEMONS.

Brett strode into the Cinephiles screening room in the basement of Hopkins Hall and inhaled one of her favorite smells in the whole wide world: hot, buttered popcorn. She couldn't wait to curl up next to Sebastian in the comfortable movie theater seats and steal hot, buttered kisses from him when the lights were dimmed. Already, half the campus seemed to be packed into the screening room. Ryan Reynolds and some guys from the soccer team jostled for position in the coveted center of the theater's rows of reclining leather seats while a pack of sophomore girls giggled at their antics. Clearly, everyone was thrilled to be off probation. Brett pictured Sebastian's hand on hers, his mouth moving close in the darkened theater . . .

"How great is this movie going to be?" Rifat Jones came to a stop beside Brett in the entryway. Her curly black hair was tied up in a ribbon, and her long, dark legs looked even more impressive than usual in gray suede peep-toe Dolce Vita ankle boots and a sleeveless violet-colored Hanii Y dress. Brett suddenly felt underdressed in her black skinny J Brand cords and peacock blue cowlneck sweater. They were watching a movie, for God's sake, not going to dinner at Le Petit Coq, the fanciest restaurant in Rhinecliff.

"Have you seen it before?" Brett asked. "It's really old. My parents used to talk about it when I was little."

Love means never having to say you're sorry, her mom would sometimes quote at their ornate marble dinner table in Rumson, New Jersey. *Unless you're the man,* her father would say, like they were a comedy routine. *Then it means* always *having to say you're sorry.* Brett and her sister, Brianna, would roll their eyes at each other while their parents laughed like it was the wittiest thing they'd ever heard.

Somehow, hearing her parents riff on the movie had not inspired Brett to Netflix it herself.

"I've never seen it," Rifat said with a wave of her hand. She smiled conspiratorially. "I'm much more interested in *who* I'm seeing the movie with than *what* I'm seeing!" She jutted her chin out, indicating Teague Williams, the good-looking senior swim-team captain, who was waiting for her near the refreshments table with a big smile and a bag of Twizzlers. Rifat gave Brett a conspiratorial wink, then turned her attention to her date.

Brett scanned the room as she searched for a seat. Rifat wasn't alone—there were certainly some new couples on display tonight, sitting next to each other or chatting shyly—like Alison Quentin and the famously aloof Parker DuBois or Kirin Choate and some baby-faced freshman Brett couldn't even name. Ugh. Who decided Perfect Match was a good idea?

"Did I miss something?" Tinsley asked in a low voice, walking over to Brett and handing her a Diet Coke. Her curtain of nearly black hair blended with the rich black sweater dress she wore over chunky motorcycle boots. The dress looked like it had been designed for Tinsley specifically, which Brett knew meant it probably had. "When did a movie in the screening room become date night?"

"Perfect Match events start tonight," Brett said, frowning. She made a face and clenched the icy-cold Diet Coke can between her hands. "Does it really have to ruin the *entire* week?"

Tinsley scanned the rows of leather seats, noting with distaste that a lot of people seemed to be having fun with their matches. Her gaze traveled over far too many laughing, joking, delighted Owls, searching for one messy golden brown head. She finally picked out Heath from the crowd—but he wasn't alone. Sitting right beside him, her glossy curls still loose and wild around her shoulders as she leaned in to giggle at whatever Heath was saying, was Little Miss Two Faces herself.

"At least your date isn't—" Tinsley began, but then cut herself off.

Because Sebastian was sitting on Isla's other side. Tinsley heard Brett's sharp intake of breath.

For a moment, both girls stood there, taking in the view. Sebastian and Heath were taking turns tossing popcorn into the air for Isla's benefit. She leaned forward to try to catch every piece, displaying her cleavage each and every time she moved.

Heath and Sebastian's interest in Isla had nothing to do with the skintight fire-engine red Rag & Bone sleeveless sheath she wore, Tinsley thought sarcastically. Clearly, she was stimulating them intellectually. When Isla laughed, Heath and Sebastian both exploded in a chorus of laughter. When she spoke, they both leaned closer and hung on her every word—so close that they could probably identify which shampoo she used and how much Frédéric Malle Outrageous! perfume she'd dabbed on the cleavage she kept flashing.

Tinsley was so infuriated that her nails dug into her palms, leaving little crescent-moon marks. How could Heath be fawning all over that girl instead of checking out Tinsley in her biker boots? Ordinarily, he could be depended upon to notice her from half the quad away. Tonight he didn't even glance up. She might as well still be out in the cold, picking up trash, for all the attention she was getting.

The movie still hadn't started, and as more and more people crowded into the screening room, some were forced to take seats along the edges of the theater. Tinsley fumed. She was in danger of being forced into standing room only while Isla had popcorn fed to her by Heath? She studied her nails for a moment, as if entranced by the matte charcoal shimmer of her Zoya Dovima polish, until she was slightly calmer.

But when she looked up again, she saw Brett still staring straight at Sebastian and Isla. Her green eyes narrowed and a bright flush highlighted her cheeks. She looked like she was about to climb over the seats and start throwing punches. Which might have been entertaining, but a fight would no doubt backfire and leave Isla once again smelling like roses.

"You look about as thrilled with this little display as I am," Tinsley managed to say through gritted teeth.

"Why doesn't she just make out with him already?" Brett asked, fuming. "It would be quicker! She's already practically sitting in his lap!"

Tinsley blinked. It had never occurred to her that other people might hate Isla as much as she did.

Which gave her an idea.

"I think you and I need to put our heads together," Tinsley said, linking her elbow with Brett's and leaning in close, so no one could overhear.

"About what?" Brett asked distractedly, her gaze still fixed on Isla and her hopelessly devoted admirers.

Tinsley nodded her head at the trio. Heath now had his arm stretched out along the back of Isla's seat, while Sebastian leaned over the armrest he shared with her—both of them grinning while Isla told a story. Tinsley narrowed her eyes. Isla had to pay. Isla *would* pay, if it was the last thing Tinsley ever did. "I think it's time we taught her how things work here at Waverly, don't you?"

Brett turned then and met Tinsley's gaze. The determined expression in her green eyes was fierce.

"Let's do it," she said.

JennyHumphrey: I'm already at the *Love Story* screening! I got us great seats in a darkened corner. ;) And I even brought snacks!

IsaacDresden: Sorry. I can't make it tonight. C U tomorrow?

A WAVERLY OWL IS NEVER TOO CAUGHT UP IN THE PRESENT TO FORGET ABOUT THE PAST.

Jenny tossed her phone into her messenger bag and flopped back against her seat, completely disappointed by Isaac's text. She'd come early to the screening just to stake out the best, most private seats in the entire Cinephiles screening room. She'd had to fight off several seniors, Celene Colista, and Benny Cunningham to keep her spot. And now Isaac wasn't even coming?

She took a deep breath and blew it out slowly, trying to calm herself down.

Toward the front of the screening room, all of her friends were together, obviously having a blast, while Jenny felt lonelier by the second. Tinsley and Brett were whispering in each other's ears. Alison Quentin looked half-nervous and half-thrilled to be sitting so close to that mysterious hottie Parker DuBois. Even Kara Whalen was laughing with Ryan Reynolds—when she wasn't giving him skeptical looks. Meanwhile, Jenny was essentially in movie theater Siberia. At least she had a giant bag of Cool Ranch Doritos and two cupcakes that she'd liberated from the dining hall. Unfortunately, she also had the sudden, self-pitying urge to eat all of it by herself. So much for a romantic night. Her date for the evening was officially vanilla buttercream frosting.

Jenny sighed and stretched out her diminutive legs. She wore a red wool miniskirt over black tights and her flat black Steve Madden fold-over boots. She'd paired it with a black-and-tan plaid Nanette Lepore jacket she'd found marked down to almost nothing in a bargain bin at Bloomingdale's and an embellished white tank from Anthropologie. To top it all off, she'd let her curls spill in wild abandon down her back and had carefully applied just a hint of Callie's Chanel Black Jade eyeliner around her brown eyes. What a waste of a cute outfit. She might as well have worn her pajamas. Which, she decided, she was going to do, stat. She'd go home and have herself a little pity party with her snacks and her sudden bad mood. She sat up, ready to make her escape.

"Is this seat taken?"

Julian McCafferty appeared before her, tall and shaggy-haired and wearing that cute smile she'd fallen for all those months ago. For a moment, Jenny had a sudden, perfect memory of Julian's soft lips pressed against hers out at Miller Farm back in the fall. She could feel the cool night air teasing her skin and that giddy, catapulting sensation in the pit of her stomach, that sense that everything was about to change. But just as quickly she remembered everything that had happened since then: how Julian had lied to her—well, failed to mention the fact that he'd been with Tinsley. She'd been so hurt when she'd found out, she couldn't look at him the same way.

But Jenny was with Isaac now, so maybe things had worked out the way they were supposed to. She didn't harbor any bad feelings toward Julian anymore. Which was just as well, since he was, supposedly, her Perfect Match.

"It's all yours," she said, waving at the seat next to her. She was glad to have the company. "Please."

Julian sank down into the seat and stretched out his long legs. He wore dark wash True Religion jeans with shredded holes at the knees. Knowing Julian, the holes were probably not for fashion but from wear. He unzipped his Everlast hoodie to reveal a faded Thelonious Monk T-shirt. He smiled at her, his easy, teasing smile that revealed the dimple in his cheek. Jenny relaxed against the back of her seat.

"How's it going, Match?" he asked. Jenny couldn't help sitting up a little bit straighter.

"I had no idea you were so into Britney Spears, my top musical influence," she teased. "That must be how they matched us up."

"She's a personal passion of mine," Julian replied at once, completely deadpan. "I loved the insouciance of her 'Oops! . . . I Did It Again' period but have been very much impressed with her recent resurrection with the 'If You Seek Amy' phase."

"Plus she still looks pretty hot in a Catholic schoolgirl outfit," Jenny said, giggling.

"Yeah, that too." Julian settled back in his seat and put his battered black Converse sneakers up on the seat in front of him. Down in front, faculty members waved lingering Owls toward the seats that remained, and the overhead lights flickered in warning. "So I hear the Three-Legged Race is the favorite Valentine's week Perfect Match activity."

"It is?" Jenny had been more interested in the romantic kissing possibilities at the movie and the ball. But then again, she'd entertained those fantasies when she'd been convinced that she and Isaac would be each other's match.

"Some of the guys in my dorm were plotting out strategies for winning." Julian shrugged.

"A three-legged race requires strategic planning?" Jenny asked, laughing. Only at Waverly. She tried to imagine her classmates at Constance Billard even *discussing* a three-legged race and couldn't. No way.

"Heath Ferro was telling everybody at lunch that he has a secret recipe for a certain Three-Legged Race Iced Tea," Julian said, tapping his fingers against his legs as if drumming along to music in his head. "Without any iced tea in it, of course. He says the goal is to booze up as much as possible and then blame any falling down on the race, not the drinking." He grinned. "But he would say that."

"I like winning more than drinking," Jenny said with a little shrug. "But then again, I don't see why we have to choose between the two."

Julian's eyes met hers, and he nodded.

"You are a girl after my own heart, Jenny Humphrey," he said, his brown eyes twinkling.

Jenny laughed. "We are going to dominate the race," she said. "Especially if everyone else is staggering around trying to recover from Heath's iced tea."

"I think we should take a bait-and-switch approach," Julian said, leaning in like he was imparting deep, dark secrets and didn't want anyone to overhear him. "I think we *pretend* to get loaded on the iced tea and then smoke everybody straight off the starting line. *Then* we enjoy the iced tea—as, like, a victory drink. Homemade Waverly champagne."

Jenny tapped her fingers against her chin, like Dr. Evil mulling over a plan for world domination. "We'll already have an advantage," she mused. "You're so tall and I'm so short that no one will think we'll be able to pull it off."

"Bait and switch," Julian said again, laughing. He put his palm in the air. "High five, Match. I think we're going to kick some ass."

Jenny smacked his palm with hers as the lights started to go down. As the room darkened and a few Owls started applauding, she realized with some surprise that planning their three-legged-race strategy with Julian had actually taken her mind off Isaac.

At least, for the moment.

A WAVERLY OWL DOES NOT ENTERTAIN

MULTIPLE SUITORS.

Callie stretched in her comfortable leather recliner and propped her feet up. She admired her weathered tan Marc Jacobs ankle wedge boots for a moment, then made sure the huge bag of popcorn she'd been unable to resist was still held securely between her knees before tipping her head back so she could see the huge Cinephiles screen completely unimpeded.

"If you push back even farther," Alan St. Girard said from beside her, "you can, like, almost tip over into the ceiling."

Obviously, he was stoned. He was always stoned. But Callie pushed back anyway and giggled when she saw that he was right, stoned or not: if she tilted her head back as far as she could, she felt like her recliner was almost in free fall. Trust Alan to have discovered something like that.

"How many movies did you watch in here before you figured

that out?" Callie asked, turning her head sideways so she could look at Alan, the most random "perfect match" of all time. Exactly what did they have in common? Her occasional use of herbal tea to soothe a sore throat and his all-day, everyday love for herbal refreshment didn't really scream *compatible*.

Alan grinned, his hazel eyes sleepy, and crossed his arms over his faded-to-gray North Face hoodie. It had a hole in one elbow and several bleach stains.

"Um. One?" He shrugged. "I like to lean."

Callie was still giggling when she felt someone sit down on her other side. She twisted around to look and felt her breath catch.

Easy.

He wore his familiar, paint-spattered, worn-in Levi's and threadbare black sweater, but his short hair reminded her this wasn't the Easy of old times.

"Hey," she said softly.

"Hey." He didn't smile, though his dark blue eyes seemed to glow. "You want to share that popcorn?" he asked. "I'm hungry." He looked past Callie and tipped his chin in the universal male sign of greeting at Alan. Alan flashed him a peace sign in return and settled back in his seat with his hands behind his head.

"Help yourself," Callie murmured to Easy, indicating the popcorn she held on her lap. And whatever else he wanted. Like maybe her heart.

Easy smiled slowly, and Callie's toes curled in her boots. And then the lights dimmed above them, and the screening room went totally dark.

The movie flickered upon the screen, and Callie watched, but she could hardly make sense of what she was seeing. She registered plaintive piano music, snow, and brick buildings that reminded her of the Waverly campus, but that was about all she took in. All of her attention was focused on Easy. He sat so close beside her that she could smell the faint hint of the Irish Spring soap he used, and she could feel the heat of his muscular shoulder against hers.

"Thanks for the popcorn," Easy murmured into her ear. His hand brushed hers inside the cardboard bucket, and their eyes met—then held.

Callie looked away first, feeling suddenly shy. Or maybe she just couldn't believe that Easy was really here, right next to her with his dark blue eyes fixed so intently on hers.

Callie watched a few more minutes of the movie, still not really seeing anything. She was suspended in a dream where there was nothing but Easy and the rest of the world had fallen away entirely. Hours could have passed. Days, even. But she was snapped out of her trance when Alan suddenly jerked up and stood up from his seat.

"Are you okay?" she whispered. Alan usually moved slowly.

"This dude's voice is tripping me out," Alan said, gesturing at the screen. "I'm out of here."

He nodded a good-bye in Easy's direction and then took off. Callie watched him go, noticing for the first time that it was standing room only along the walls of the screening room. A flash of guilt washed over her when she saw that Brandon was one of the people standing there. She had ignored a call from him earlier, not to mention a few texts. She hadn't felt like talking to him . . . because she didn't know what to say. She didn't know what to do. She bit her lip and noticed he was standing with a very geeky-looking girl she'd never seen before.

The girl's awful plaid skirt and ugly glasses looked almost silly next to Brandon's perfectly worn-in APC New Standard jeans and a black Pringle cashmere zip-front sweater with stand-up collar and oxford gray stripe across the chest. Talk about an odd couple. She almost laughed when she realized that the girl had to be Brandon's Perfect Match.

Brandon's eyes caught Callie's from across the room. He pushed away from the wall and came over to slide into Alan's abandoned seat, leaving his match without a backward glance. Suddenly Callie found the whole thing a lot less funny. With Easy on one side and Brandon on the other, she'd been thrust back into last night's dream. Except this was real. It just involved hot, buttery popcorn instead of sweet red grapes.

Callie kept her eyes trained on the movie screen and bit back a nervous little giggle. She reached into the bucket for more popcorn, not sure what else to do.

Brandon brushed against her fingers with his as he grabbed a handful. Then, seconds later, Easy did the same.

Nobody spoke.

Callie suddenly found herself wondering if a girl could actually die from sensory overload. She felt as if her skin was too tight, like it was stretched too thin over her body. She could hardly manage to catch a full breath. It was awful and wonderful at the same time.

And then, suddenly, Easy and Brandon both jerked back—and Callie realized that the two of them had touched each other's hands rather than hers in the popcorn bucket.

Easy glared at Brandon's perfect, unwrinkled sweater that looked like it belonged on a male model and his hair gelled *just so*. Why had he even come over here? Why couldn't he leave Callie alone? Easy dug his fingers into his jeans and reminded himself that the guy was still technically with Callie. He glanced at her out of the corner of his eye. She was staring straight ahead at the screen, her jaw set, tugging on a strand of her wavy strawberry blond hair—which she did whenever she was stressed out.

Easy leaned back into his seat and tried to focus on the movie. Ryan O'Neal was carrying his wife over the threshold of their new apartment, but Easy didn't care. His mind was racing. Why was Callie stressed? And why hadn't she broken up with Buchanan yet? She'd had plenty of time to do it today. . . . Did she not want to?

Brandon could not believe that Easy Walsh was lounging in the seat next to Callie like a moody, blue-eyed flashback. He did not like the way the night was going. At all.

First he'd been waylaid by Cora on his way into the Cinephiles screening room. The girl had turned out to be as hard to shake off as a barnacle from the underside of one of his dad's boats. She would not stop talking—so Brandon had missed his opportunity to find Callie before the lights went down. He'd seen her sitting with her Perfect Match, Alan, which was fine, but he hadn't seen Easy Fucking Walsh until Alan had left and he'd taken his spot.

And now Callie wouldn't even look at him. She wouldn't snuggle up to him or hold his hand. She shot a look at Easy, and Brandon felt the same old jealousy seep through him. He gritted his teeth. *No way,* he thought stubbornly. There was *no fucking way* that Callie would do this to him again. She'd told Brandon repeatedly that Easy was in her past—but, something inside him whispered, now that Easy was back from playing soldier, all bets were off.

No. He refused to believe it. She wouldn't—couldn't—do this to him, not again.

But he wasn't about to take his eyes off the two of them, just in case.

Callie stared straight ahead, afraid to look at either boy. What had she been thinking? She couldn't handle the two of them at once. She could hardly handle one of them at a time! She'd been with Brandon sophomore year when Easy had swept her off her feet, and she was technically with Brandon now—and, more to the point, the previous night when she'd made out with Easy outside Dumbarton. This messed-up love triangle had been plaguing her for years. But she couldn't be with them both at once. She had to choose.

Callie blew out a breath. Her dream had very quickly become a nightmare.

OwlNet   Instant Message Inbox

HeathFerro: The Three-Legged Iced Tea is primed and
                  ready! Bring your flask and tell your friends.

RyanReynolds: On. It. And what is up with your ex gf? She
                   was cool at first but got kinda crazy because I
                   talked during the movie last night. That movie
                   sucked ass!

HeathFerro: Mention her to me again and you're cut off.

RyanReynolds: Dude. Chill.

HeathFerro: You know the rules. Break them at your peril.

SageFrancis: I hear Heath made a vat of something toxic.

BennyCunningham: God, I hope so!

SageFrancis: Want to head over there and get some before the race this afternoon?

BennyCunningham: You know it! Remember last year? I had three sips of whatever he made and did a header two jumps off the starting line. Too funny.

SageFrancis: I need to get wasted so I can block out Drew Gately. How is he my match???

BennyCunningham: Ew. He's so gross. You can have some of mine if you need it.

SageFrancis: Promise me you'll pick me up if I pass out on the ground. You know he won't!

BennyCunningham: I have your back.

IsaacDresden: Hey there, Match. I was wondering if you wanted to come over this afternoon before the Three-Legged Race? My sources tell me it's a lot more fun with some cocktails, and I can get us into the wine cellar here. I know the dean. ☺

BrettMesserschmidt: I like the sound of that! What time? I get out of calc at 2.

IsaacDresden: I'll meet you right after that on the quad?

BrettMesserschmidt: C U then!

10

A WAVERLY OWL KNOWS WHEN TO MIND HER OWN
BUSINESS—AND WHEN TO MIND SOMEONE ELSE'S.

Brett stuck her hands into the pockets of her navy double-breasted coat and buried her chin against the blue-and-black plaid Armand Diradourian scarf her sister, Brianna, had sent her as a part of her latest care package from New York. Ahead of her, Isaac led the way up the steps to the dean's house. His house.

The last time Brett had been here, she'd stormed off from the infamous Jan Plan party, furious with Sebastian. That memory did not exactly inspire her to be any more excited about *this* visit. But Isaac was really nice—he'd met her on the quad as promised and they'd had a nice walk over—and Brett really could go for a glass of wine to get her mind off his bitchy, boyfriend-stealing sister. She didn't know why she'd been paired up with Isaac. He seemed sweet, but as far as Brett could tell the only thing they had in common was that they both liked Jenny.

She walked up the steps behind him as he tugged off one of his brown leather gloves and flipped open the box that concealed the security pad beneath. She watched him tap a very long string of numbers into the machine.

"Wow, that's some door code," she observed. "I can't remember more than four numbers at a time."

"Neither can I," Isaac said, grinning over his shoulder. "Which is why the password is my birthday and then my sister's, so we'll all remember it. My dad gets pissed if we have to call security just to let us into the house."

Brett smiled at him and followed him into the foyer. She glanced up at the stained glass cupola, which glowed prettily in the afternoon sunshine. The dean had had it repaired almost immediately after the party, Brett had heard. You'd never know that Isla had crashed through it—and had somehow survived to continue ruining lives.

Brett pulled off her scarf, shoved it in one of her pockets, and followed after Isaac as he headed toward the kitchen in the back of the house. He shrugged his coat off and tossed it on one of the benches in the small eating area, so Brett did the same. She smoothed her hands over her hips. She'd dressed for the Three-Legged Race in dark midnight blue J brand cords, shiny black patent leather Repetto ballet flats, and a charcoal gray hip-length Inhabit cardigan with chunky buttons. She fingered one of the buttons as she stood in the kitchen, amused for some reason that even in the dean's fancy residence the ancient Waverly radiators kept up their symphony of hissing and clanking. It was the same in Dumbarton.

"Let's get the pregame going," Isaac said with his cheerful, open smile, and pulled on the door on the wall nearest him, waving Brett through. "I've been waiting forever to really christen this wine cellar. Probation lasted way too long."

"Tell me about it," Brett agreed, although she wasn't sure exactly how much Isaac, as the dean's son, had actually suffered. She was pretty sure *he* hadn't had the questionable joy of being restricted to a dorm and then only let out for academic reasons, usually monitored by a member of the faculty.

"I missed Jenny," he said as he led the way into the cool cellar. Brett felt herself soften. How sweet was this guy? He'd hated not seeing Jenny as much as Brett had hated not seeing Sebastian for all that time. Though Brett was pretty sure Sebastian wasn't telling Isla all about how much he'd missed Brett.

She shook her head and forced herself to forget about Isla for a few minutes. How often was she going to find herself in the dean's fully stocked wine cellar? It was a dim, concrete-floored space filled with wooden racks teeming with elegant bottles. She shouldn't let Isla ruin this, too.

Isaac selected a bottle from one of the racks in front of them, then pulled it out and set it on the little table in the middle of the cellar. When she moved closer, Brett saw that the table had been made from a weathered wine cask turned on its side.

"I hope that's a good one." Brett nodded at the wine bottle. She felt grown-up, standing in a dimly lit wine cellar with a good-looking guy who she knew wasn't about to make any kind of move on her. It was like one of those scenes from her future life she might have dreamed about back when she had been in eighth grade and desperate to get to boarding school.

"It's a nineteen ninety-two Screaming Eagle cabernet," Isaac said. He grinned. "My dad has like ten cases. He won't even notice it's missing." He deftly opened the bottle and poured the rich, red liquid into two glasses. He put down the bottle and picked up his glass. Brett did the same.

"To Perfect Match," she said, because it felt like the right moment for a toast.

"Perfect Match," Isaac said. They clinked their glasses together, and then Brett took a long sip of the wine. It was rich and smooth and warmed her instantly.

"Nice," she said. She kept herself from laughing again, because what did she know about wine? Brett was never sure if she actually liked wine or only wanted to like wine. But she definitely liked the *idea* of wine—and she really liked how holding a red wineglass in her hand made her feel. Like she was Lady Brett Ashley from *The Sun Also Rises*, maybe, instead of Brett Messerschmidt from Rumson, New Jersey.

"My dad can be kind of annoying sometimes, especially when he's doing his whole 'dean' thing," Isaac said, rolling the stem of his wineglass between his palms. "But he definitely knows his wine."

Brett settled in on a small stool beside the table, deciding to take notes for Jenny. Isaac was such a gentleman—so friendly and sweet, not at all like so many of the usual jerky, obnoxious Waverly guys. Jenny had completely lucked out. Brett felt loyally that such luck was well-deserved, especially after Jenny's string of boys gone wrong: Easy, Julian, Drew. Isaac was obviously the one worth waiting for.

"We were pretty happy at our old school," Isaac said. "But I have to say, I'm psyched that Waverly is turning out to be even better."

"Of course," Brett said, confident that they weren't really talking about the school. "There's a reason so many people love this place. It's just . . . better than other places, you know?"

Isaac's eyes met hers, and his lips twitched into a smile. "It really is," he said softly.

They were just finishing up their second glasses of wine, Brett's brain full of gushy things to tell Jenny about her man, when they heard footsteps from up above—and the unmistakable trill of Isla's laughter.

Isaac looked up toward the ceiling and brightened. Brett forced a smile.

"Must be my sister," he said, like Brett hadn't guessed.

Isaac grabbed a couple bottles of wine and headed for the stairs, and Brett reluctantly followed. Why was he in such a rush to hang out with his sister? Didn't he see her all the time? Shouldn't Isaac be the one guy at Waverly who *didn't* think Isla was all that?

Upstairs, Brett paused in the kitchen doorway. Sebastian was leaning against the counter, an indulgent smile on his face as he gazed down at Isla. She was perched on the tall bar stool next to him, looking entirely too sexy in a Juicy Couture vest with a faux-fur hood, a tight turtleneck that showed off her curves, and a tight pair of dark Rock & Republic jeans.

Brett involuntarily balled her hands into fists and cleared her throat.

"Oh," Sebastian said, when he realized they were no longer alone. He smiled at Brett but didn't move away from the counter. "Hey. I didn't know you were here."

"I told you I was coming over to Isaac's before the Three-Legged Race," Brett said stiffly. Why hadn't he mentioned that he would be there with Isla? He'd had ample time to do so at lunch before Brett had run off to her calculus class, but he hadn't said a word.

"We're prepping for the race," Isla said, waving a half-full Svedka vodka bottle at Brett. "Are you seriously going for wine?" Her pale green eyes latched on to the bottles in Isaac's hands. She sounded scandalized, but Isaac shrugged.

"Clearly we're more civilized than you are," he teased.

Isla wrinkled her pert, ski-jump nose at him. "Are you headed over there?"

"Soon," Isaac said, holding up the wine bottles in his hands.

There was a brief, very tense silence as Isla doctored two take-out coffee cups and handed one to Sebastian, who kept his eyes trained on the drinks. He didn't feel Brett's glare on the side of his face or see the way her jaw was clenched with fury. Of course he didn't. He was far too entranced by Isla.

"Let's do this," Isla said. He took a sip and shuddered theatrically. Isla giggled, and Brett resisted the urge to throw one of the wine bottles at her. Isla could tell Brett was jealous, she was sure of it. Ironic how the girl Brett hated the most was more aware of her feelings than her own boyfriend.

"It's like paint thinner," Sebastian said. He grinned at Isla. "It's perfect."

Finally he crossed over to Brett but only to give her a measly peck on the forehead, like he might give to his eighty-five-year-old grandmother.

"See you," he murmured, and then he and Isla swept off into the afternoon.

Together.

Brett blinked into the sudden emptiness of the kitchen, not sure how she was supposed to react.

"We need to conceal this somehow." Isaac frowned at the wine bottles he held, oblivious. He set the bottles down on the counter and tossed his phone and keys beside them. "I think I have a Nalgene bottle upstairs. I'll be right back."

He ran up the stairs, and Brett tried to talk herself down from her fury. Sebastian and Isla were just doing the Perfect Match thing. There was no need to freak. How many times was she going to get upset about this kind of incident? So far, every time she'd freaked out about something, she'd been wrong. When was she going to learn to trust him?

A little buzz emitted from Isaac's BlackBerry. Brett had the overwhelming urge to check his messages, just to see. It wasn't for her, she told herself, it was for Jenny. She wanted to give her friend a full and accurate account of all of her boyfriend's adorable traits—and who knew? Maybe this was a text message from the Rhinecliff florist, announcing some huge delivery to Jenny. She glanced toward the ceiling, as if she could see through the walls and track Isaac's movements.

Brett moved across the room and picked up Isaac's phone, clicking open the chat bubble. It was the latest in an ongoing conversation.

MollyWagner: Hey sweetie. What's the V-Day deal? Are you still coming to visit?

IsaacDresden: I don't know yet. I'm trying to work it out . . .

MollyWagner: Don't tell me those Waverly girls have eaten you alive. ;)

IsaacDresden: Nothing like that. I just have a lot going on.

MollyWagner: What's more important than your girlfriend and Valentine's Day???

IsaacDresden: I know, I know. I'm a terrible boyfriend.

MollyWagner: That hasn't been determined yet. But good thing U R cute!

Brett dropped the phone like it was on fire and stared at it as it clattered against the granite countertop. *Isaac was a liar. And a cheater.* She heard a noise behind her and whirled around to see Isaac standing there with a Nalgene in each hand, smiling and looking triumphant.

Isaac, who until three seconds ago, Brett had thought was the perfect boyfriend.

She couldn't help glancing over at his phone instead of meeting his gaze. He looked, too, and then color swept over his cheeks and stained his neck as he looked back at Brett, realizing what she'd seen.

"I'm going to break up with her," Isaac said after a long, tense moment. His voice sounded thick. Brett couldn't quite meet his eyes. Any buzz she might have had from the wine was gone. She felt faintly ill instead.

"Just . . . please don't tell Jenny," Isaac said, his voice pleading. "I just—I need to tell her about this myself, okay? It's complicated."

Brett crossed her arms over her chest and nodded stiffly. It wasn't her place to tell Jenny, and she certainly didn't want to be in the middle of this mess. She knew about cheating, after all. She'd cheated on her old boyfriend Jeremiah. She hadn't wanted him to find out the things he'd found out—and certainly not in the way he'd found out about them. An "I Never" game was the worst possible way to learn your girlfriend had cheated.

She knew it was complicated. It was always complicated. She just wished she'd kept out of it. This was nothing she wanted to know.

Poor Jenny, she thought as she wrapped her scarf around her neck and threw her coat back on, still not quite meeting Isaac's gaze. There she'd been, thinking Isaac was so sweet and so nice, and the truth was that he was lying and cheating the whole time. Dating poor Jenny and leading this other girl on, too.

Suddenly Brett felt completely justified in her jealousy of Isla and Sebastian. Guys were obviously capable of anything.

You just never knew.

11

A WAVERLY OWL KNOWS THAT GOOD IDEAS CAN COME FROM UNLIKELY SOURCES.

The Waverly Field House was filled with Owls in varying states of obvious intoxication, and the volume was reaching fever pitch. Matched couples were scattered about, figuring out how to tie themselves together with the regulation rope bindings for the Three-Legged Race. Callie and Alan stood a little bit back from the starting line of the current heat of three-legged competitors, watching the mayhem unfold. Verena Arneval and her tall, geeky senior match hobbled for three wobbly steps and then collapsed, her partner squashing her into the AstroTurf of the Field House grounds.

"Heh. Face-plant," Alan said from beside her, laughing. "Ten points!"

Callie smiled but said nothing. She had yet to uncover one single thing she and Alan had in common, but by now she'd come to appreciate their pairing's randomness.

Reason number one for this newfound appreciation stood on one side of the crowd, his dark blue eyes brooding and stormy whenever they landed on Callie. Which was roughly every three seconds. Reason number two stood almost directly opposite, his leg tied to the geekiest girl to ever wear a maroon Waverly blazer. Easy. Brandon. Easy. Brandon. Callie felt like she was watching some kind of Ping-Pong competition as her head swung back and forth between them.

Easy caught her eye from where he stood, arms crossed, just watching her. His dark brows rose, like he expected her to do something—and she knew exactly what that something was. After all, she'd promised, hadn't she? Callie swallowed. And then, against her will, she felt her head pulled around to find Brandon's gaze on her—just as troubled and just as dark.

Callie felt her breath go shallow. She hadn't even had more than a sip or two from Alan's flask, but her head was spinning.

"Christ," Alan said, looking at her with a bemused sort of alarm. "Are you okay? You look like you're tripping the hell out."

"I just . . . I can't . . ." Callie felt the Field House walls closing in on her, as if she were being gripped and squeezed by a giant, sweaty fist. Alan threw down the rope he'd been halfheartedly trying to tie into a decent knot and took Callie's elbow.

"Forget this," he said. "Let's get out of here. I have a much better idea."

Easy stared at her from off to the right, Brandon from the left.

Callie knew she was a coward, because she dropped her gaze and let Alan usher her far away from them both. He led her outside, where the snow had started to fall again. It wasn't until they'd reached the coffee bar in Maxwell that she was able to breathe normally. She let Alan direct her to one of the comfortable couches in the deserted student hangout and sank down into the plush cushions. She closed her eyes, breathed through her nose, and willed herself to be calm.

"Here." Alan plunked a large coffee in front of her and flopped down next to her on the couch.

"Um, thanks," Callie said. She pushed her strawberry blond waves back from her face and unzipped her royal blue Michael Kors coat, letting it fall off her shoulders. She didn't know what kind of coffee Alan had bought, but it didn't matter. Anything would do. And if she needed anything stronger, she knew where he kept his flask.

As she picked up the cardboard cup, Alan dug in one of the interior pockets of his coat. He pulled out a ziplock baggie, opened it, and then grinned at her.

"Brownie?" he asked.

Callie raised an eyebrow. She didn't have to ask what was in it. This was Alan St. Girard.

"I thought you were a smoker," she said. "When did you turn into Rachael Ray?"

"I like edibles," Alan said, still grinning. "It's a natural progression. It attracts significantly less teacher attention and makes a great mid-class pick-me-up."

Callie decided she didn't care. Maybe her life would make

more sense if she viewed it from the Alan St. Girard perspective. *He* was certainly never in danger of succumbing to a panic attack, was he? Hardly. She accepted the proffered brownie and took a huge bite. She expected it to taste like dirt and weeds, but it didn't. Chocolaty goodness exploded on her tongue. She sighed happily. "Betty Crocker would be proud."

"It's all yours," Alan said, pulling out a second brownie for himself. "Bon appétit."

They both settled back against the couch, and finally, slowly, Callie relaxed. She could feel the tension gradually leaving her body with every breath she took. It helped that Maxwell, usually overrun with Owls and the very last place anyone would ever go to relax, was like a ghost town tonight.

"Everybody must be at the Field House," she said after a while. "Maybe to escape the snow."

"Waverly is falling down, falling down, falling down . . ." Alan sang to the tune of "London Bridge." He was wearing a tie-dyed T-shirt from Ben & Jerry's that read CHERRY GARCIA, and suddenly Callie couldn't stop giggling.

She visualized Easy and Brandon as Three-Legged Race partners, bound by the legs and hating each other but grimly soldiering on toward the finish line—only to collapse in a tangle of limbs. All to the tune of Alan's ridiculous song.

She collapsed against the back of the couch, laughing uncontrollably. Alan laughed, too.

"I don't even know what you're laughing about," he said after a few moments while Callie wiped tears from her eyes.

She regarded Alan for a moment. He was scruffy and silly

but really one of the nicest guys she knew. She had the sudden
urge to spill everything to him. It might be the best idea she'd
ever had, or at least a much better idea than many of the ones
she'd had recently. It wasn't just because of his special brownies, either. He was Easy's roommate and friend. And he was also
friends with Brandon. And unlike some of the other guys—like
Ryan Reynolds or Heath Ferro—he wasn't likely to use anything she told him against her. That just wasn't his style.

"Well?" he asked. "Should I sing a different song?"

"It's Easy," Callie said. "And Brandon."

Alan blew out a breath, as if he'd just climbed up a huge
hill. He shook his head. "Yeah," he said. "That's . . . a whole
thing."

"It really is," Callie agreed with a sigh.

Before she knew it, the whole long, tortured saga poured
out of her. She and Alan were the only people in the whole of
Maxwell, and their little couch felt like a safe little oasis from
the drama of her life. She told Alan everything, going all the
way back to when she and Easy had started making out in the
rare books room in the library at that party at the beginning of
sophomore year, even though Callie had been dating Brandon
at the time. She went over every single excruciating detail of
her relationship with both boys—well, not *every* detail—and
she didn't spin the story to make herself look any better.

As she talked, she played with the edges of her open, cream-
colored Joie cardigan and the belt loops of her brown Theory
slim-legged cargo pants. It was as if she couldn't sit still. And
when she was finished telling Alan all of her secrets, she felt

much better. It was like finally getting her legs waxed and her eyebrows shaped after letting it all go for far too long—she felt smooth and clean.

"Whoa," Alan said after a few moments. "That's some intense shit."

"I know," Callie said, and suddenly she was giggling again. "But it's my life."

Alan laughed. "I guess you're stuck with it, then."

"I guess." She let her head fall back against the couch. "What would you do?"

Alan shifted his position on the couch with a thoughtful frown. He stuck his long legs out in front of him and shoved his hands into the pockets of his Diesel jeans. "I would go back in time and choose one of them," he said, after a moment or two of intense consideration. "With no overlap."

Callie sighed and closed her eyes. If only time travel were an option. Unfortunately, Alan's brownies weren't *that* powerful.

"But I get that you can't exactly do that," he continued. "It's like the three of you are caught in a vicious circle. Like it's an undertow, and none of you can get your heads above water."

Callie tugged harder at her belt loops. She pictured Easy and Brandon caught in the pull of the ocean off some deserted beach, tossing and turning in the waves, and she could save only one of them. She looked at Alan. "That's exactly what it feels like."

Alan shrugged. "So you break the cycle," he said matter-of-factly.

Callie frowned. "How do I do that?"

"You break up with *both* of them," Alan said, stroking his beard. "The way you should have years ago. Then you wait and see who fights the hardest for you."

"They're not going to fight each other, Alan," Callie said, rolling her eyes.

"They would if this was a Bruce Lee movie," Alan replied immediately. He shook his head, as if to clear it of images of martial-arts masters. "But that's not what I mean. You watch and see who fights for you. In, you know, a nonviolent way. Whoever that is, well, that's the one you're meant to be with."

Callie stared at his goofy stoner grin and his kind brown eyes. She thought about how helpless she felt when Easy was around. He was like a fire she could never quite put out. And she thought about how good Brandon was to her, how understanding and sweet, never angry or demanding. And she thought about how little she wanted to hurt either one of them yet again.

Alan might possibly be the most brilliant person she'd ever encountered.

"Oh my God," she breathed. It was all clear to her. Finally. "Thank you, Alan!" she cried, and gave him an impulsive hug.

"You got it," he said, grinning.

Callie flopped back against the couch and couldn't help smiling. Because for the first time since she'd walked into the foyer at the dean's house and seen Easy Walsh standing there surrounded by broken glass, she had a plan.

BrettMesserschmidt: If you're still in for Operation: Isla Takedown, I have a major breakthrough to report . . .

TinsleyCarmichael: I am so in. That overdressed liar offends me with every breath she takes.

BrettMesserschmidt: I can get us into her house. Yes, the dean's house, site of all our pain. Tomorrow?

TinsleyCarmichael: Let's get this party started.

A LITTLE HEALTHY COMPETITION IS GOOD FOR A
WAVERLY OWL.

"It's all in the knees," Julian said with mock-seriousness, demonstrating his three-legged technique by dropping into a squat every other step, throwing his arms out as if he were surfing, and pretending not to notice the spectacle he was making of himself in the middle of the Field House.

"You realize that everyone is staring at you, right?" Jenny asked, trying to stifle a giggle. Students were packed into the bleachers that ringed the interior of the Field House, waving maroon Waverly banners and wearing Waverly sweatshirts in support of the race, like it was a varsity event.

"They're trying to figure out my secret." Julian held Jenny's gaze as he dropped into a particularly low squat. Jenny couldn't help it anymore and burst out laughing. She was pretty sure it wasn't thanks to Heath Ferro's wicked concoction. *That* had already taken out two sophomore girls, at least four freshmen, and one unwise senior soccer player who'd reportedly chugged four entire pint glasses of the stuff in Richards before staggering his way up to the Field House. He'd puked all over a goalpost and was now sleeping it off beneath the bleachers.

Julian stopped his squat walk, and the two of them headed for the makeshift winner's circle near the starting line. A race was still in progress, with the usual level of mayhem and silliness. Alison Quentin and Parker DuBois were hobbling down the racecourse, teetering and tottering like a seesaw. Verena Arvenal and her senior partner couldn't walk more than two steps without falling over—which made him angrier and angrier while Verena only laughed. Only Jenny and Julian had managed to keep their cool. They'd won their preliminary heat by following the strategy they'd plotted out the night before at the movie screening. No one had expected them to make it this far.

Jenny waved excitedly at Brett and Isaac as they walked over, having also just won their heat. That meant they got to stand with Jenny and Julian in the winner's staging area, waiting for the final match that would determine the overall winners of the big race.

"Welcome to the finals!" Jenny called out as Brett and Isaac approached the winner's circle together. Brett looked tense, her shoulders rigid and far too close to her ears. Next to her, Isaac was walking in that easy way of his, his maroon hoodie zipped up over a button-down shirt, with the tails hanging over his dark-washed jeans.

And then he grinned, his smile lighting up his whole face as his gaze met Jenny's. A familiar rush of warmth rolled through her as his green eyes held hers for a long, delicious moment. There was nothing weird or distant about that grin. Had she been giving her imagination a workout lately? Had she made the whole thing up? Jenny smiled at him and stuck her hands in the pockets of her Lucky cords.

"You looked okay out there, Dresden," Julian said carefully, as if discussing an NFL game with a member of the opposing team. He frowned and crossed his arms over his chest. "But we're about to enter the finals. Looking good isn't going to win you anything here in the big leagues."

"Whatever," Isaac retorted in the same tone. He moved from Brett's side and put his arm around Jenny's shoulders. He smiled down at her, and the look in his eyes was affectionately teasing. "Jenny barely comes up to your knee!"

"Low blow!" Jenny cried.

"No pun intended," Brett said dryly.

Jenny laughed, and caught Isaac's eye. She was glad she hadn't called him the night before to ask what was going on. Clearly, nothing was. Her brother, Dan, always told her that guys were simple and direct. *If he said he was busy, it's because he was busy.* Maybe one day she would start listening to him. Maybe.

"All right, Owls!" cried Miss Friedman, the phys ed teacher known for her sadistic insistence on four hundred sit-ups at the first hint of any infraction of Waverly policy. She climbed up onto one of the lowest bleacher seats, sending a few wide-eyed freshmen scrambling out of her way. She was tall and thin,

with one of those short, blunt haircuts that reminded Jenny of
geometry exercises. "It's time for the final race! All qualifying
teams, please line up and tie yourself to your partner."

Isaac squeezed Jenny's shoulder before he stepped away,
relinquishing her to Julian. Jenny was sure it was the look he
gave her as he walked toward Brett that made her stomach feel
fluttery—and not the way Julian moved close to her side and
pressed his leg against hers. She looked down at him, taking in
his wavy hair and the faint smell of soap and sweat. She flexed
her leg against the rope, checking to see how tight it was.

"Trust me," Julian said, looking up at her, his golden brown
eyes warm. "I'm good at this stuff."

For some reason, Jenny felt her breath catch. Maybe it was
the weird sensation of being this close to Julian again. Maybe it
was just some kind of physical déjà vu.

"Better tie that tight," Brett said, snapping Jenny out of her
trance. She made a face at Jenny. "She's so little, you might step
right over her without noticing it."

"Ha-ha," Jenny replied, rolling her eyes.

Brett caught her eye and mouthed the word *kidding*. Jenny
smiled back, having taken no offense. This was a competition—
and competitions meant some trash-talking. She'd been known
to do her share of it from time to time on the hockey field or
with her family. It was a time-honored Humphrey family tradition. She smiled to herself, thinking of how even Rufus abandoned his usual principles of love and peace to talk trash during
a competitive Scrabble game.

"Jenny and I have a foolproof system," Julian continued,

grinning at Jenny as he straightened. He wrapped his arm around Jenny's back, assuming the competitive three-legged stance. Jenny slid her arm around his waist, trying not to notice how taut his back muscles were. Next to them, Brett and Isaac linked up, but a bit more gingerly. "You underestimate us at your peril."

"Still not scared," Isaac tossed back at him with a grin. "Brett and I don't need a system, because neither one of us is freakishly too tall or too short."

"We're like a well-oiled, same-sized machine," Brett added.

"Whatever," Julian said dismissively. "I have the best partner ever!"

"I know you do," Isaac agreed, and the look he gave Jenny then made her cheeks heat up.

"Hey!" Brett said, pretending to be annoyed at Isaac. She elbowed him in the side, hard enough to make him wince. "You have a pretty amazing partner yourself. And I'll remind you that you're tied to me. If I trip, we both go down."

"He doesn't mean it," Jenny told her, laughing. "You know he has to say it—total boyfriend law."

Brett looked over at her and frowned. Jenny felt a flash of panic—was it too soon to call Isaac her boyfriend? But then the starting whistle blew, and there was no time to think.

The race was on!

She and Julian fell back into their rhythm, which essentially consisted of Jenny clinging to his one leg while he made a medium-size stride, then anchoring them while he made a huge, long stride with the full reach of his other leg. Jenny felt a little bit like a monkey clinging to the side of a tree—though Julian was a very good-looking, very athletic tree.

"Your head is not in the game," Julian chided her when they were about halfway down the racecourse. He had to shout over the din of the Field House, which echoed with screams and cheers and silly songs from the watching Owls.

"Of course it is!" Jenny giggled. "Go, J-squared!"

"Totally lame," Julian replied, but he was laughing, too.

Two of the couples near them crashed to the ground, having swayed too close together and getting overbalanced. It was Jenny's job to navigate Julian's long stride around such obstacles, like a coxswain in a crew race.

"Go left! Go left!" she cried, acting like the pivot as Julian moved around the senior couple's tangled limbs. His long legs ate up the ground beneath them, leaving Isaac and Brett far behind.

Step, pivot. Step, pivot. The kids in the stands cheered and screamed. The Waverly band was blaring out a marching song. Jenny looked up at Julian, and his lips curved into a smile. His arm tightened around her back, and she dug her fingers into his side. And then they crossed the finish line!

"We rule!" Julian shouted in triumph. Jenny looked around wildly to see two couples in thrashing piles on the ground. Isaac and Brett, each wearing fierce scowls of concentration, were just approaching the finish line. She whipped her head around and realized that no one was ahead of them. They'd won!

"Your Three-Legged Race champions, ladies and gentlemen!" Miss Friedman cried into her bullhorn. "Jenny Humphrey and Julian McCafferty!"

Jenny whooped for joy and hugged Julian around his lean waist. She felt a little buzz shiver through her limbs and laughed up at him. He grinned down at her. Jenny leaned back to wave at all the Owls in the stands who were stamping their feet and cheering. She was as proud as if she'd climbed Everest. And all she'd had to do was hang on!

Julian untied their legs and was still grinning down at her when Isaac and Brett crossed the finish line behind them.

"Your legs are way too long, man," Isaac said, glaring at Julian in mock anger. "They should be outlawed, like steroids."

"Nothing makes me happier than a sore loser," Julian replied, grinning.

"This sore loser needs a drink," Brett declared, fanning her face. The boys took off to grab waters from the nearby school-sanctioned refreshment table, and Jenny watched them go, her eyes lingering on Isaac's cute little swagger of a walk. She pulled out a tube of Urban Decay lip gloss in her favorite color, Quiver, and applied it to her lips, rubbing them together.

"You're lucky we're friends," she told Brett, sliding the tube back into her pocket. "Or I might have to be a little jealous that you got to spend all that time essentially hugging Isaac in front of the entire school. You'll be happy to know I trust you both."

She expected Brett to laugh, but instead she frowned. Jenny bit her lower lip and studied her friend's face.

"What's the matter?" she asked when Brett didn't say anything. But Brett didn't meet her eyes. She shook her head, her bright red bob sliding forward like a curtain to hide her face.

"Nothing," she said.

"You're, like, scowling at your shoes," Jenny pointed out. She didn't want to push Brett or anything, but she had a weird feeling that whatever Brett was frowning about had to do with her.

"I don't mean to be," Brett said. She looked at Jenny then, her green eyes serious. "I just think you shouldn't get ahead of yourself." She nodded over toward Isaac, who was already on his way back, Julian right behind him. Isaac's head barely cleared Julian's shoulders. "You know? Maybe you should just . . . see where it goes."

Jenny opened and closed her mouth, like a goldfish. What was *that* supposed to mean? Was Brett . . . *warning* her?

But she lost her chance to ask, because Brett put on a smile for the boys, and Jenny had to gulp down her panic and confusion and do the same.

BrettMesserschmidt: Emergency! I think I left my chem textbook in your kitchen yesterday before the race!

IsaacDresden: NP—I can get it to you later this afternoon. I'm about to walk into history class, but I can swing back home afterward.

BrettMesserschmidt: Shit. I have chem in fifteen minutes and our teacher is a hardass about not having the textbook . . .

IsaacDresden: No worries. We keep a spare key under the mat outside the kitchen door. Just use the code: 1-0-1-9-0-7-2-9

BrettMesserschmidt: You're awesome. Thank you!!

13

A WAVERLY OWL ALWAYS BEGINS A RESEARCH
PROJECT USING PRIMARY SOURCES.

"Check you out," Tinsley said admiringly when Brett threw open the Dresdens' back door with a little dramatic flourish. She kicked the key under the welcome mat with her black Coach riding boots. "You're like a spy."

"I always wanted to be a spy," Brett said with a giggle as she stepped into the dean's house and paused, listening for any sounds. She opened her oversize gray Stella McCartney coat as she strained to hear something from the depths of the house. She knew that Dean Dresden was attending a function in New York City that day, and Mrs. Dresden was usually off-campus during the day, but you could never be too careful while breaking and entering. *If you have the key, does it count as a felony?* Brett wondered as Tinsley closed the door behind them.

The Dresdens' house was silent, save for the faintest hiss from the radiators and the usual noises of an old house settling around them. There were no sounds of any people who might wander into the kitchen and discover Brett and Tinsley. Any slight bit of guilt that Brett might have felt—and it was the barest sliver, growing smaller every time she recalled the sight of Isla and Sebastian flirting in this very kitchen—was completely washed away when she thought about Isaac's secret girlfriend and how she'd had no choice but to keep quiet about her around Jenny yesterday.

She straightened her shoulders and moved farther into the house. Why should she feel guilty? Obviously, the Dresdens had some genetic flaw that made them all liars and cheaters and who knew what else. Brett felt, as a member of the Disciplinary Committee and an active part of the Waverly community, that it was her *duty* to expose the evil siblings for who and what they really were. She *owed* it to Waverly.

And if it made Sebastian think twice about hanging on Isla's every simpering word, well . . . that was just a happy bonus.

Tinsley suffered no pangs of guilt whatsoever. Picking up her fellow students' trash for a month in the freezing cold because of Isla's lies completely canceled out any wrongdoing she might commit today, she thought as she marched through the kitchen and headed directly across the first floor toward their real destination: Isla's ground-floor bedroom. It was time to snoop.

She pushed open the heavy wood door and entered Isla's room. The first time she'd been in there, she'd thought it was weird that a girl who seemed so badass—so, frankly, like herself—would live in a bedroom with a big, girly four-poster bed, complete with tons of lace and Pepto-Bismol pink walls.

Now, however, she narrowed her eyes and thought that maybe, just maybe, the discrepancy was a clue she should have heeded way back when—before she'd basically *allowed* Isla to take her down so easily.

"My God," Brett said, walking through the door behind Tinsley and stopping dead in her tracks. "Which American Girl doll threw up in here?"

"I was thinking more like Disney Channel," Tinsley said, her hands on her hips as she slowly turned a circle in the center of the room. Her gaze drifted over the Waverly calendar on the wall to the antique dresser to Isla's stack of schoolbooks on the rolltop desk. "Because I definitely get a little bit of a Hannah Montana vibe."

"Explain to me how someone who channels Angelina Jolie while getting herself breakfast in the school cafeteria can sleep well in this room," Brett said, sounding personally affronted. She stared at the bed. "Is that *Laura Ashley?*"

"That," Tinsley said, "is exactly what we're here to find out."

Brett pulled out her phone and checked the time while Tinsley unzipped her loden green Prada puffer jacket and tossed it carelessly onto the bed.

"I confirmed that Isaac is in class for the next hour," Brett said. "There's no chance he'll show up here until after that."

"And I checked Isla's schedule online," Tinsley said. "She has back-to-back classes all afternoon." She smiled serenely when Brett looked at her, a question in her eyes. "People who plan to backstab other people should take care to change their e-mail passwords before they decide to throw down. That's all I'm going to say."

"Excellent," Brett said, her lips twitching into a smile.

They got down to business. Brett took on the bed area, reaching under the pillows and deep into the crevice between the mattress and box spring, searching for anything incriminating. Instead, she found what you could reasonably expect to find in any dorm room on the Waverly campus: an almost-empty bottle of Absolut Citron and a half-smoked joint. Nothing that would help to incriminate Isla in any grand sense. Though Brett wasn't above getting Isla in regular old trouble with her parents, if that was all they came up with. She turned her attention to the bedside table, opening the drawers and paging through Isla's worn copy of *The Bell Jar*.

"Apparently, she might be depressed," Brett said with a sigh, waving the book at Tinsley, who was sitting at Isla's desk, rifling through the drawers.

"How eighth grade and angsty," Tinsley said, rolling her violet-colored eyes. She opened her mouth to say something else but then froze, her hand landing on a leather-bound book. "Now this is what I'm talking about," she breathed. She flipped open the small book and, as she took in the handwritten pages, felt victory flood through her, actually warming her up from the inside.

Gotcha, she thought with intense satisfaction. Isla Dresden was indeed dumb enough to make Tinsley Carmichael her enemy—*and* keep a diary.

"Is that what I think it is?" Brett asked, her green eyes lighting up.

"It certainly seems to be." Tinsley shifted over in the chair in front of Isla's desk as Brett pushed in beside her. Together they flipped through the pages, sitting so close that Tinsley could smell the faint eucalyptus scent of Brett's favorite La Mer moisturizer. It made Tinsley irrationally happy, like if she closed her eyes she might be back in Dumbarton 303 with Brett and Callie a year ago, before she'd been kicked out for doing E and before everything got so complicated.

"Who hides a diary in an easily accessible desk drawer?" Brett asked. She frowned at it. "Isn't she afraid someone will read it? Like her brother?"

"Maybe Isaac is trustworthy," Tinsley said, flipping open the book and making the pages flap—so loud that she almost missed Brett's derisive snort. Tinsley looked at her questioningly.

"We're here to find dirt," Brett said, nodding solemnly at the diary. Obediently, Tinsley dropped her gaze to the handwritten pages in front of her. But she filed away the knowledge that Brett wasn't so impressed with *either* Dresden sibling. *Interesting.*

"Blah blah blah," Tinsley narrated, her eyes scanning the entry in front of her. "I've never understood why people write in these things. Why ask questions of a piece of paper? It's not going to answer you. And besides, you can just walk outside and actually *do* something instead of writing about things that already happened."

"Waverly isn't what I expected," Brett read aloud, ignoring Tinsley. *"Dad hates it when we say we're basically like military brats,*

but it's true." She stopped and looked at Tinsley. "Please tell me that the most evil girl on campus is not actually, secretly, this boring? And yet has somehow managed to play you *and* me?"

Tinsley shook her head, refusing to accept that idea. What could she possibly do with a secret like that? *Isla is painfully dull* didn't have quite the same ring as *Isla is a heroin addict* or *Isla sniffs glue* or even *Isla is known to have slept with every last guy at her former school, student* and *teacher.*

Determined to find some dirt, she continued to flip through the pages, stopping at a more recent entry. Isla's handwriting was wide and loopy and required a moment or two to decode.

I don't know what I'll do if anyone finds out, she'd written. *I'll have to switch schools again, at the very least. I've worked so hard and even done things I'm not exactly proud of, and all of it was to make sure that NO ONE at Waverly could ever find out.*

"Promising," Brett said, reading along over Tinsley's shoulder.

I would DIE, Isla's loopy script continued. *I would just DIE if anyone knew—*

The front door slammed shut from out in the hallway, and both girls jumped. The diary fell from Tinsley's hand, back into the desk drawer where she'd found it.

"Shit!" Brett hissed, jumping to her feet. She sneaked over to the door and peeked out. "It's Mrs. Dresden," she whispered, her eyes wide with horror. "We have to get out of here!"

Tinsley took a last regretful look at the diary, slid it back beneath the pile of papers she'd found it under, and stood up. She snatched her coat up from the bed and threw it on as she walked over to Isla's window.

"Okay," she whispered, frowning. "Small problem with that."

She pointed outside, where last night's freshly fallen snow lay pristine and untouched beneath Isla's window. They would leave tracks, and that was bound to make *someone* suspicious. So much for the easiest escape route.

"What's the likelihood that she won't even look out the window?" Brett asked in a whisper from Tinsley's side. Her brow was furrowed into a deep frown. "I don't look at the ground outside my bedroom window every time I walk in the room, do you?"

"You know today would be the day she did," Tinsley muttered. She led the way back to the door of Isla's bedroom and eased it open, ears pricked for the sounds of Mrs. Dresden as she moved through the house. The kitchen sink came on, then was turned off. *Click, click, click* went the woman's heels against the hard kitchen tiles.

"We have to wait until she goes upstairs," Brett whispered. Tinsley nodded.

There was silence for a while as Tinsley and Brett stood like statues, afraid to even breathe. They heard the clank of cutlery. The Sub-Zero refrigerator opening and closing. The rattle of ice cubes in a glass, then the distinctive snap and hiss of a soda can being opened. Meanwhile, Tinsley was all too aware that the clock was ticking—that any other Dresden could appear at any time, like the dean himself, who was certainly no Tinsley Carmichael fan. She was going to have to come up with a Plan B.

The sound of Mrs. Dresden's heels echoed down the front

hall again, growing louder as they came closer. Brett's fingers dug into Tinsley's arm, and they each held their breath as they waited to see if Mrs. Dresden would head toward Isla's bedroom. Tinsley's mind raced. Would she hide under the bed or in the closet? Or should they just jump out the window and let Isla convince herself she had a stalker?

But instead of moving toward her daughter's room, Mrs. Dresden turned and started up the stairs to the upper floor.

Tinsley and Brett stared at each other in amazement at their luck. *Fucking saved,* Tinsley thought, adrenaline pumping through her. Brett covered her mouth to keep from laughing in sheer relief. They had to get out of there before they both lost it.

They sneaked out of Isla's room and then eased their way across the hardwood floors that seemed to creak and groan at top volume beneath them. Twice, they froze—convinced that Mrs. Dresden would hear them and demand to know who they were and what they were doing—but both times there was no sudden outcry from above.

"When we get to the front door," Tinsley whispered, "we have to open it and then run for our lives."

She took a deep breath and threw open the front door. The bright winter sun flooded inside, and the chilly wind howled in her face. They stepped outside and Tinsley eased the heavy door shut behind her.

"Let's go!" Brett hissed, and then they were running— exploding with pent-up energy from hiding, giddy and still one shout away from being busted.

They skidded down the front walk and around the brick wall that contained the dean's property and only stopped running when they made it to the main path of the quad. Tinsley gasped for breath and grabbed Brett's arm. They slowed to a calculatedly casual stroll. They could be anyone. Walking anywhere.

The mission hadn't been accomplished, but it also hadn't failed. And it certainly wasn't over yet.

14

A WAVERLY OWL IS WILLING TO CONSIDER ANY

REASONABLE PLAN OF ACTION.

Callie stood in the rare books room of the Sawyer Library, looking out over the campus. The sun reflected off the snow and made the bare branches of the trees on Hopkins Hill seem to glitter. But she couldn't really appreciate the scenery.

She crossed her arms over her chest and hugged her brown and melon-colored Milly turtleneck dress closer to her body. She tucked her chin inside the turtleneck, stretching it slightly, and let her waves of strawberry blond hair fall forward to spill over her shoulders. The more she thought about what Alan had said, the more she was positive that he was right.

She hadn't acted on his advice that night—she'd been too busy giggling and consuming her body weight in dry Cap'n Crunch cereal from the Maxwell dispenser. It had never tasted so good before, which was exactly why she didn't like to get stoned very often. She ran her hands over her hips, making sure she hadn't bloated up like an inflatable raft.

Callie's eyes scanned the deserted, cozy rare books room, but she didn't see what was in front of her—she saw scenes from her past. Easy kissing her, right here, for the very first time back in sophomore year. Making out with Brandon just last month and getting caught by his Swedish girlfriend over the webcam. It just went on and on and on, and Callie had no idea how to end it. Or, worse, how to make a decision.

Which was why Alan's plan was so perfect. *She* wouldn't have to make the decision at all. She could let Easy and Brandon figure it out. Whoever fought the hardest for her was the one she was supposed to be with. It was like that King Solomon story her mother, the governor of Georgia, brought up whenever she had to make decisions she knew would anger her constituents. In the story, the two mothers argued over a baby, each saying it was hers, until King Solomon declared he'd cut the baby in half. The *real* mother leaped forward to protect the child, relinquishing her claim, and in so doing proved that she was the true mother. That was more or less what Callie had to do. Sever herself from both guys—and see who proved himself to be the right one.

Callie took a deep breath. She dug her Treo out from the depths of her red Jimmy Choo patent-leather hobo bag and stared at it for a moment. She would never normally break up with someone over e-mail, but this wasn't normal, was it? Nothing about this was normal.

And the truth was, she wasn't entirely sure she could look into Easy's dark blue eyes the way she had on the top of the

Empire State Building and break up with him all over again. The same way she didn't think she could *watch* herself crush Brandon's feelings under her heel, the way she had so many times before. So maybe she was a little bit of a coward. At least she was doing *something*.

The ends justify the means, she thought. She had to do what she had to do. For all of them.

From: CallieVernon@waverly.edu
To: EasyWalsh@waverly.edu
Date: Wed, February 11, 12:33 pm
Subject: Re: Us

Easy,
I'm really sorry to do this over e-mail.
I just don't think it's going to work.
I'm sorry.
Callie

Before she could think better of it or change her mind, Callie hit SEND.

Then, gnawing on her lip and completely obliterating what was left of her Preserves Hint of Honey Lip Therapy gloss, she sent the exact same e-mail to Brandon.

She let out her breath and felt something like a head rush. It was done.

Now all she had to do was sit back and wait. Wait to see which one of them really loved her, after all.

IsaacDresden: I think you left your scarf in my living room last night. Did you do that on purpose? ;)

JennyHumphrey: It's like a trail of breadcrumbs . . .

IsaacDresden: It's working. I feel the overwhelming urge to have lunch with you today.

JennyHumphrey: Done. See? The scarf has magical properties.

IsaacDresden: I thought that was you. ☺

SebastianValenti: Earth to missing girlfriend. Where are you?

BrettMesserschmidt: What are you talking about? I saw you last night . . .

SebastianValenti: For five minutes. Maybe three minutes.

BrettMesserschmidt: For dinner, which is more than five minutes. Do you need more tutoring??

SebastianValenti: If I say yes, will you cut class and come hang out with me?

15

A WAVERLY OWL IS RARELY TAKEN BY SURPRISE.

Brandon heard the beep of an incoming e-mail on his laptop and sighed. He knew who it was, and he couldn't deal. He had roughly twelve seconds left to finish his English paper and about five minutes after that to race across campus to class.

He definitely did not have time for another one of Cora's e-mails.

"Brandon's got a stalker. . . ." Heath singsonged from across the room they shared. Brandon glared at him. Heath, naturally, looked completely at ease as he pulled on a long-sleeved black and red Lacoste rugby shirt and ran his hands through his messy, shaggy dirty blond hair. That was the entirety of his morning routine. Because Heath, unlike Brandon, didn't care if he looked like he'd slept in his dirty-wash Diesel jeans. Or maybe they were regular-wash jeans that Heath just hadn't bothered to take to the laundry room yet. With Heath, you never knew.

Brandon glanced down at his own Rock & Republic jeans and freshly laundered Hugo Boss hoodie to confirm that he hadn't absorbed his pig of a roommate's dedication to filth through dorm-room osmosis or something.

"You need to tell Queen of the Dorks that you're busy," Heath continued, unaware of or unaffected by the dirty look Brandon was giving him. "Like, permanently busy."

Brandon rubbed his hands over his face. Heath was right. "She won't leave me alone," he muttered.

Heath smirked. "And now you know what it's like to be me," he said with a happy sigh. "My little boy is all grown up!" He smiled almost sweetly. "Of course, I *was* matched with Tinsley. Looks like I'm just destined for hotter things, unlike a geek magnet like you, bro." He shook his head. "So sad."

Brandon shook his head, too and turned back to his computer. He should have known better than to discuss anything with Heath of all people. He did know better. The fact was, Cora really *was* driving Brandon crazy. She didn't seem to understand that as far as Brandon was concerned, Perfect Match was a finite collection of required—not desired—events. It didn't mean Brandon was suddenly dating her or even suddenly friends with her. But no one seemed to have mentioned that to Cora. It was only Wednesday morning, and already he'd had to turn down an invitation to study together, to eat breakfast together, to go into the town of Rhinecliff together. *Thanks, but no thanks.*

He didn't necessarily want to be a dick about it, the way he knew Heath would be without a second's hesitation. Brandon wasn't like that. He refused to be like that—what would be next? Would he wake up to find he really had transformed into a degenerate asshole who couldn't even be bothered to shower half the time?

He clicked to open the e-mail, resolved to be nice yet again. It didn't really cost him anything to just be nice, after all. But the e-mail wasn't from Cora. It was from Callie.

Brandon read it once. Then again. Then, because it still didn't make any sense, one more time.

But the words didn't change. Callie was dumping him. Again.

"Callie just broke up with me," he blurted out, too shocked and stunned to do anything else. At least this time she sent an e-mail, he thought. It was better than, for example, walking into a room to find her kissing someone else.

"Shit, man," Heath said. He moved to the hook on the back of their door and wrapped his ratty black scarf around his neck, obviously done with the conversation. Brandon instantly regretted telling him about the e-mail at all, even involuntarily. Heath shrugged into his charcoal Shipley & Halmos peacoat and grabbed his messenger bag from the floor, where he'd tossed it the day before. Homework was one more thing Heath didn't really do unless he absolutely had to.

"Later," Heath said, and opened their bedroom door.

Brandon's head was spinning—and he was pretty sure he was just too numb to feel what he ought to be feeling, so wouldn't *that* be fun when it caught up with him—but he did know that the last thing he wanted was for the whole school to be talking about what a loser he was, *again*. That Callie had ripped his heart out, *again*.

"Hey," Brandon said. "Don't mention this to anyone, okay?"

Heath gazed at him innocently. "Of course not, buddy." He smiled. "Your secret's safe with me."

A WAVERLY OWL KNOWS THAT GOOD NEWS

TRAVELS FAST.

Easy was daydreaming through his history class, which was much more entertaining than paying attention. Farnsworth Hall was famous for being one of the most overheated places on campus. Even though the windows were wide open, the room felt like a broiler. He was approximately five hundred degrees and had been forced to strip down to his thinnest layer, a battered Jimi Hendrix concert T-shirt he'd worn under his henley and hoodie. Directly beneath the windows, Kara Whalen had her coat and hat on and was still shivering. Easy thought the waste of all that energy was more interesting than another discussion of the New Deal, but he knew better than to say anything. Ms. Harrigan's teaching style was more Attila the Hun than Earth Mother.

He missed his history class from fall semester. At least then he'd gotten to stare at Callie while he doodled in his notebook

and imagined he was riding Credo through the fields somewhere, with Callie sitting behind him, clinging to his waist
and pressing up against him. This semester he had to have the
fantasy without the visual aid. Still entertaining, if a little bit
less fun.

Easy looked up, startled, when Heath Ferro slid into the seat
next to him. He wasn't even in this class. Easy nodded in greeting, but instead of returning the gesture Heath leaned toward
Easy as he took off his coat.

"Did you hear?" he asked, a bright gleam in his green eyes.
Easy knew that look. It generally meant trouble.

"Hear what?"

"Callie dumped Brandon," Heath said, watching Easy
closely. Too closely. "Harsh."

For the first time since he'd been sent away back in the
fall, Easy was actually grateful that he'd had some experience
with military school. He might not have learned the respect
for authority his father had claimed he would, but he'd very
quickly learned how to compose his expression to complete and
utter blankness. Not easy to do with a drill sergeant barking
in your face. He stared back at Heath and didn't so much as
twitch.

"Excuse me, gentlemen." The sarcastic tone of Ms. Harrigan's voice cut in. "I don't mean to interrupt your conversation,
but are you new here to Waverly?" The teacher scrutinized
Heath, propping one hand on her round hip.

"Actually, I'm an important part of the establishment,"
Heath replied, lounging back in his desk chair and gazing at

Ms. Harrigan as if she had not, in fact, been chastising him. "Pleasure to make your acquaintance. Heath Ferro."

Everyone laughed, and Easy couldn't quite help the smile that threatened to take over his mouth. Not because of Heath's stand-up routine but because of the news he'd just delivered.

Finally.

Finally, Callie was free. He couldn't really believe she'd done it—she'd let Buchanan go. Which meant . . . everything would finally be the way it was supposed to be. He could kiss her whenever he wanted. He could have her all to himself. He could walk out of Farnsworth Hall the minute this class was over, go find Callie, and make her stand in the middle of the quad while he demonstrated exactly how he felt about her.

Only thirty minutes to go.

After Heath slid out of the classroom, saluting Easy and accepting a round of applause, the rest of the class passed in a blissful kind of blur. It was much easier to fantasize about Callie when the fantasy would soon be a reality. When class was finally over, Easy didn't retain a single fact about the New Deal or Franklin Delano Roosevelt. But he knew where he was headed, and it wasn't to another boring lecture. He would convince Callie to blow off her afternoon classes, and then maybe they could act out some of his favorite fantasies. He could hardly wait.

As the class streamed out around him, he stood up and dug his phone out of his pocket to text Callie and see where she was. He didn't care what she was doing, really, he just wanted to be with her. It was like he'd finally admitted that there was an empty space inside him that only she could fill—and he couldn't stand being apart from her for even one second more.

As he exited the class he looked down at the blinking message indicator, then clicked over to his e-mail. He smiled. She'd already e-mailed him. They always thought of each other at the same time, like there was some invisible cord tying them together. Subject: *Us.*

Easy opened up the e-mail and felt his mouth drop open. He stopped dead in the middle of the bustling hallway.

I just don't think it's going to work.

She was . . . breaking up with him?

They weren't even officially together. She'd broken it off without giving him a chance. A second chance. Or were they on their third or fourth chance? He couldn't remember.

He felt like she'd punched him in the stomach. What the hell?

BennyCunningham: I just heard that Callie dumped Brandon!

SageFrancis: Again?! WTF?

BennyCunningham: I can think of only one reason, and his initials are E.W.

SageFrancis: Um, then why did I just see him looking like he wanted to punch a wall outside Farnsworth?

BennyCunningham: Huh. Sounds like another episode of Unsolved Waverly Mysteries . . .

AlisonQuentin: Isn't there some love poem thing tonight? Do you think I should see If Parker wants to go?

CelineColista: Only if you hate him. Or want him to hate you. Or just want to die together, surrounded by extreme lameness.

AlisonQuentin: Really? Ryan Reynolds told me he heard it would be cool?!

CelineColista: That's Ryan pretending to be sensitive. Kind of like how he pretends not to be a man-slut. . . .

HeathFerro: Callie Vernon is single again. You gonna hit that or what, Perfect Match?

AlanStGirard: Dude, so not my type.

HeathFerro: Right, because you hate hot girls. I forgot.

AlanStGirard: She's hot, for sure. But too high-maintenance.

HeathFerro: I think the hotness outweighs any personality issues, personally.

AlanStGirard: You think that about everything that moves.

HeathFerro: True.

AlanStGirard: Hey, what's up for tonight? There's some poetry reading?

HeathFerro: Did you put crack in your weed? I'm going to pretend you didn't ask me that.

17

A WAVERLY OWL ALWAYS LISTENS TO THE VOICE
OF REASON.

Jenny decided on a bright red bowl of tomato soup with a side of roasted red pepper bruschetta for dinner on Thursday evening, after eyeing something that claimed to be red beans and rice but looked a whole lot more like reddish brown oatmeal. She took a small helping of the beet salad, just to add some vegetables to her existence, but shuddered at the salmon mousse on rye toast. She shoved her tray along the track, biting her lip as she tried to choose between red velvet cupcakes and strawberry ice cream sundaes with raspberry sauce—neither of which she *wanted* necessarily. But this was her first Valentine's Day at Waverly, and she thought she should get into the mood. Red velvet cupcakes it was.

The dining hall certainly had. There were red streamers hanging from the walls and shiny red hearts on every plastic tray. Red Kool-Aid sat in large pitchers near the drinks machine, and pink-tinted Rice Krispies Treats were stacked on platters near the rest of the desserts. Red Jell-O sat in a large glass bowl, wobbling slightly, next to separate bowls of cherries and strawberries. It was red, red, red, as far as the eye could see.

Including Brett's signature fire-engine red bob, which Jenny spotted the moment she walked into the dining hall. Jenny had told herself over and over that it didn't matter what Brett had said on Tuesday at the Three-Legged Race. Isaac had been back to his normal self since then—and Jenny was almost entirely convinced that the weirdness she'd sensed between them was just a little blip. She wouldn't have given it another thought if she didn't still have the echo of Brett's words sneaking around in her head, whispering *I just don't think you should get ahead of yourself* when Jenny least expected it.

Jenny had come up with a hundred explanations. Like, maybe Brett was just concerned that she was falling too hard for someone she didn't know very well. After all, she could admit, with a flush of embarrassment, she *was* sort of known for taking things too seriously, too fast. She didn't even want to think about how many times she'd been in love since the start of the school year. But still . . .

"Hey," she said in a determinedly cheerful voice when she made her way to Brett's side. Brett was still scowling at the variety of red foods, looking personally affronted by the spread.

"What's up with all the forced Valentine's Day cheer?" she asked crankily. She wore a charcoal gray wool Nanette Lepore sweater dress over opaque tights and knee-high black Elie

Tahari boots. She looked sleek and serious, and not at all interested in Red Hots or lacey doilies.

"I guess it's just something else to celebrate," Jenny murmured. Brett seemed as tense as she had in the Field House the other night, and Jenny wondered if she might just be wound up about her own problems.

"Hooray," Brett said under her breath. She bypassed the entrées altogether and picked up a dish of the wobbly red Jell-O.

"So . . ." Jenny kept pace with Brett as she moved through the serving area. "Can I ask you a question?"

"Sure." Brett slid her a look and smiled. "You just did."

Jenny grinned, but she wasn't going to be put off that easily. She had to know. "What did you mean," she began, annoyed that her voice was climbing up a couple of octaves. She coughed slightly to cover it. "You know, in the Field House? When you said . . . what you said about Isaac and me?"

Brett stared down at her bowl of Jell-O, wishing that she could disappear through the tile floor beneath her feet. Anything to avoid Jenny's wide, worried, doelike brown eyes.

Why had she said anything in the first place? She felt her temper kick into gear and wished Isaac were nearby to take the brunt of it—because he clearly hadn't told Jenny yet, the way he'd kind of promised he would. So now he was *that much more* of a liar. It was his fault she even had to have this conversation.

She didn't want Jenny to hate *her*, after all.

"What are you talking about?" she asked, looking away

from Jenny. She hated having to lie—but how could she tell the truth? It would only make things worse. Isaac could do his own dirty work, thank you very much. Besides, it was entirely possible that Isaac had already broken up with his girlfriend at his other school, in order to be with Jenny. And if that was the case, Brett didn't want to stir up drama where there wasn't any. "What did I say?"

"You know." Jenny's cheeks reddened. "That stuff about, um, getting ahead of myself?"

"I don't even remember saying that," Brett lied, and forced a laugh. It sounded as brittle as she felt. "I must have had too much of Heath's iced tea."

Jenny's big brown eyes seemed to get even wider, if that were possible, and her shoulders sagged. Brett felt like she'd drop-kicked Bambi.

"I have to go talk to Tinsley," Brett said breezily. She smiled apologetically and then quickly walked away, trying not to look like she was hurrying. She felt horrible. Jenny was her friend. But she didn't know what else to do. She wished she'd never looked at Isaac's phone in the first place.

Jenny watched Brett practically sprint away from her, weaving in and out of the red tableclothed tables. What was going on?

"What's wrong?" a familiar voice asked. Jenny turned to look up at Julian, who was wearing a friendly smile and a long-sleeved black thermal shirt that clung to his lean chest.

"Why do you think something's wrong?" she asked, deflecting the question. She forced a small smile. "Maybe I'm just contemplating the *redness* of everything." She waved a hand at the dining-hall selections that she no longer had an appetite for.

"Nope," Julian said, tucking his hands in the pockets of his cargo pants and rocking back on his heels. His gaze was warm and knowing. "I know that worried look you make."

Jenny shook her head, her brown curls bouncing up and down around her. "What worried look?"

Julian ducked his head and wrinkled up his forehead, in an imitation of her. Jenny didn't think she'd ever made that particular face, but Julian looked awfully cute making it. She couldn't help but laugh.

"So?" he asked. He took Jenny's tray from her hands and walked over to an empty nearby table. Once they were seated, he turned to give Jenny his full attention. He waited, patiently, for her to go on.

Suddenly Jenny couldn't think of a single reason *not* to tell Julian the whole story. So she did. She told him how Isaac had been acting strange before the Three-Legged Race, but now he seemed normal. And she told him what Brett had said—and how she couldn't seem to let it go.

"I don't know," she said, blowing out a breath. "I just can't help thinking that she might know something that I don't. I can't stop wondering about it."

Julian nodded, his brows drawn together in thought. He reached over, snagged a red velvet cupcake from Jenny's tray, and peeled the paper cover off its base.

"What did Isaac say?" he asked after discarding the paper. He popped the entire cupcake in his mouth, somehow still looking cute as he chewed then swallowed it. Jenny was sure she would look like a pig if she shoved a whole cupcake into her face. Maybe she'd look like one of those mini-pigs they were breeding in England.

"I didn't ask him about it," she admitted.

Julian shrugged. "If you're worried about something, you should talk to him," he said, his tone gentle but sure. "Because if it's a good relationship, you should be able to talk about anything, right? Isn't that the point?"

Jenny smiled as Julian's words moved through her like sunshine, making everything feel better and warmer as they went.

Julian was right, of course. She *should* be able to talk to Isaac about it.

Why hadn't she thought of that?

18

A WAVERLY OWL KNOWS THAT IF AT FIRST YOU
DON'T SUCCEED, TRY, TRY AGAIN.

Tinsley tossed her coat into the empty space next to
Heath at a long table full of boys and sank down into
the chair next to him. After his pathetic performance
in the Three-Legged Race the previous night—a performance
for which he was, quite literally, falling-down drunk—she felt
that on some level he owed her. She also felt compelled to mark
her territory in front of as many Owls as possible. Heath might
be kind of a slut, but he was *her* slut. Or at least, he was her
Perfect Match.

"What's up?" Heath said, eyeing Tinsley over the collar of
his blue Hugo Boss button-down. He'd shoved the sleeves up
over his elbows, the better to lounge back with his dirty blond
hair a mess and that ever-present smirk on his chiseled face.
"I'm surprised you didn't just fall down on me again, like last
night."

"*I* was not the drunken idiot who could barely walk, Heath," Tinsley drawled, sweeping her hair off her shoulder. She made sure every male eye at the table was focused on her—all eyes were, of course, except for Sebastian's, which Tinsley grudgingly allowed out of loyalty to Brett—before letting the silky strands fall out of her hand one by one, sliding and slithering over her bare shoulder. Lon Baruzza and Ryan Reynolds practically drooled into their sodas. She crossed her long legs, encased in skintight Fendi leather leggings, and let one black Prada buckled stiletto pump dangle from her foot. "That would be you."

"Please," Heath said with a laugh. "I *make* the drinks. I don't do headers on the AstroTurf."

"And yet there you were," Tinsley retorted with a mischievous grin. "Facedown on the racecourse—repeatedly—and nearly disqualified for failing to tie a knot correctly."

"I thought you were the one who sailed halfway around the world with the America's Cup when you were, like, eight years old," Heath tossed back. Tinsley smiled, satisfied that he still remembered random facts about her life. "Why was I the one tying the knots when you're supposed to be the expert?"

"Aw, Heathie, do you need help with your knots?" Tinsley practically purred. "Didn't you learn that in kindergarten like everyone else? Or should we get you some Velcro sneakers?"

Heath's grin widened as laughter swelled around the table. His green eyes met Tinsley's, amused, and he shrugged as if to say *you got me.*

Tinsley reached over and picked up one of the strawberries

she'd piled onto her plate, feeling oddly pleased with herself. Was she really having a good time with Heath Ferro? Weren't there warnings about him all over the girls' bathroom stalls on the Waverly campus? Maybe across all of New York State?

"Why don't you teach me everything you know about tying knots?" Heath suggested when the jeering had calmed down. He smiled at Tinsley suggestively. "Since bondage is apparently your thing. Feel free to demonstrate."

Tinsley opened her mouth to deliver a stinging putdown, but before she could get a word out, Heath had turned away.

Isla was sitting down on his other side, letting her tray clatter against the table and slithering into her seat with a writhing motion that had all the boys gaping. Tinsley fought back the urge to glare at the table at large. Had they all missed the lesson about eating with their mouths closed?

"Hey, Match," Sebastian drawled, smiling at Isla. Tinsley glared at him on Brett's behalf, but he didn't seem to notice.

"How did you like the Three-Legged Race?" Heath asked eagerly, like his own personal happiness hinged on Isla's answer.

"If you have the right cocktails, you can have a good time doing anything," Isla said, sending her flirty little look from Heath to Sebastian and then back again. Tinsley entertained a graphic fantasy of smashing her strawberry sundae on top of Isla's so-careless-it-obviously-took-seven-hours ponytail, and watching it drip, cold and punishing, all the way down into the bateau neckline of her emerald green Elizabeth and James tunic, until it ran down her jeans and collected in a frigid pool in her Kate Spade flats.

"That is an evil smile," Brett said in a low voice, sliding into the seat next to Tinsley. Her eyes shifted toward Sebastian before settling back on Tinsley.

"You're just in time," Tinsley said in an undertone. "Her Majesty has just decided to grace us with her presence." She arched her eyebrows, inviting Brett to join her in the Isla-hate. She felt bad that Brett's boyfriend was one of the fools slobbering over the girl, but she couldn't deny that she loved having Brett there to commiserate.

"So," Ryan Reynolds said, leaning forward and smiling at Isla, flashing his dimples. Tinsley and Brett looked at each other in disgust. "What was Valentine's Day like at your old school?"

"We make kind of a big deal out of it here," Lon Baruzza chimed in, training his dark eyes on Isla as if no other girl existed.

"Did you do anything special last year?" Heath asked, with emphasis on the word *special*.

"Oh, please!" Brett huffed under her breath, and Tinsley rolled her eyes. Talk about a lame attempt to find out about Isla's love life.

Isla played with the ends of her dark hair. "As a matter of fact," she said, drawing the words out until all the guys were leaning forward and practically falling out of their seats, "my old boyfriend, Xander, and I got some ink last year." She smiled a mysterious smile. "His is on his shoulder." She waited a beat, letting the suspense build. "But mine . . . isn't."

Brett glared at Sebastian, who was too busy sitting there,

listening and even smiling, to notice her angry stare. He'd barely glanced away from Isla when Brett had arrived at the table, and instead of a kiss or a smile, she'd received a nod of the head—the kind of acknowledgment Sebastian might give a familiar-looking freshman guy, not his *girlfriend*.

Brett was feeling more and more frustrated. After escaping the Dresden house yesterday, she and Tinsley had stayed up late in their room, doing more Isla "research" to figure out her big, bad secret. But despite combing every Web site they could think of, from Google searches to MySpace to the sites for all her old schools, they hadn't found a thing. Isla didn't even have a Facebook page! They'd given up at about 3 A.M., but Brett still couldn't sleep after that. She'd tossed and turned half the night, finally grabbing a few hours close to daybreak.

Isla laughed again and batted her eyes at Sebastian. Brett felt her temper skyrocket.

Her phone buzzed in her pocket, and Brett pulled it out. She raised her eyebrows when she saw it was a text from Tinsley, who was holding her own phone under the table, guerilla-style. Brett suppressed a smile, impressed by her friend's inventiveness. You couldn't let guys *see* you being bitchy toward other girls. They lived in a fantasy world where girls were as sweet and as nice to one another as they pretended to be. Which meant that girl warfare had to be taken underground.

Brett clicked open the text.

TinsleyCarmichael: *I might throw up.*

BrettMesserschmidt: *Tell. Me. About. It.*

TinsleyCarmichael: *But I think we have a clue to Isla's past, finally . . . How many Xanders can there be at her old school??*

Brett glanced up at her violet-eyed friend. A wicked smile was sliding across Tinsley's flawless face. Down the table, Isla was still flipping her hair, acting coy as the boys played twenty questions, trying to guess what tattoo she'd gotten—and where.

But for the first time, Brett didn't even mind. Maybe she and Tinsley would have to speak to every Xander they could find. Maybe they'd have to drive to Isla's old school and question him personally. It didn't matter. They'd do whatever it took.

BennyCunningham: Get ready for the Love at Waverly slideshow! I'm totally submitting that photo of you from freshman year when you passed out into your birthday cake.

SageFrancis: You promised me that photo was deleted!

BennyCunningham: Maybe it is and maybe it isn't. Where's that disgusting photo you took of me dancing last year? The one where I have seven chins and look like I'm about to make out with my own reflection?

SageFrancis: You know exactly where it is: a safe and secure place. Show anyone that cake face-plant picture and I'll send the one of you in immediately.

BennyCunningham: Right back at you, sweetie.

HeathFerro: I believe that the spirit of Love at Waverly is best represented by that picture of you cuddling up to sleep on Reynolds's lap in the Richards common room last semester.

AlanStGirard: Dude. I was passed out! You should ask Reynolds why he didn't move when I fell on him. Homo.

HeathFerro:: It's because you're so pretty.

AlanStGirard: Like I can't find just as many ridiculous pictures of you.

HeathFerro: Go right ahead. You seem to have forgotten that I have no shame.

RifatJones: If I have to sit through one more slideshow filled with all those annoying pictures of freshmen linking arms and hugging when they obviously met five minutes ago, I will scream!

VerenaArvenal: I hear you. But they're the only ones who can submit anything—all of our pics violate the Honor Code. . . .

A WAVERLY OWL EMBRACES GOOD ADVICE.

Brandon slumped against the back of his seat at one of the high coffee-bar tables in Maxwell on Friday morning, wishing he could disappear into the cushion beneath him. He stared at the latte in his hand, not really seeing it.

"She thinks she's a seven—check out that walk—but she's really a five. Maybe even a four. Though you have to admire the confidence," Heath was saying, eyeing a leggy sophomore girl who had the misfortune to walk in front of their table on her way to the coffee bar. Heath had been providing a running commentary about the attractiveness—or lack thereof—of passing Owls since he and Brandon had arrived twenty minutes ago. "So we'll say a five, for argument's sake."

"Uh-huh," Brandon muttered, shifting in his seat and tugging at the collar of his gray and black color-block Prada sweater. He couldn't bring himself to check out girls—or even muster up the energy to say cutting things to Heath. All he could think about was Callie's e-mail. It was pretty much all he'd been able to think about for twenty-four hours straight.

On some level, he'd known that she was pulling away from him, but he'd thought that was because they were all on academic probation. He hadn't thought she would actually *dump* him. He'd really thought they'd connected in that early part of Jan Plan, when it seemed like she was really, finally giving them the chance they deserved. Had she just been faking that? Or had it all been in his head? Had he made it all up because he'd been crazy about Callie Vernon since he first met her freshman year?

He'd tried every single thing he could think of to be the perfect boyfriend, and it still wasn't good enough for her. He couldn't help thinking the dumpage had to do with Easy Walsh, because with Callie it was always about Easy Walsh. Had Callie only given Brandon a chance because Easy was gone? He hadn't wanted to believe that. He didn't believe that.

Brandon was jolted out of his bitter little spiral when Cora threw herself into the seat next to him.

"Hi!" she exclaimed. Her dark auburn hair hung down from beneath her multicolored homemade-looking knit cap, and her huge brown eyes looked way too hopeful behind her dark-rimmed glasses. She wore a puffy pink jacket open over a bright turquoise sweater and jeans that bagged in the wrong places even while she was sitting down.

Brandon forced a polite smile. The irony. Callie had to be coerced into spending time with him even when she was his girlfriend, but his stalker wouldn't leave him alone.

"Hey, Cora," he said weakly, all too aware of Heath's sudden intense interest. He'd actually stopped leering at girls to watch Brandon deal with his Perfect Match.

"Cora!" Heath cried in evident delight. He smiled wickedly and leaned closer, propping his elbows on the table. "I have heard *so* much about you," he continued sweetly.

"Oh," Cora said, blinking at Heath as if he were a different species. Which pretty much showed that she was far more discerning than Brandon had given her credit for. "You have?"

"Of course I have," Heath assured her, gazing at her intently. "My roommate's Perfect Match is obviously someone I need to know. Intimately."

"Ignore him," Brandon told Cora. "Seriously. He's mentally deranged."

"Brandon's just a little cranky," Heath said, still smiling innocently. "He's really not much of a morning person."

"I'm not, either," Cora said. She swept her lashes down to cover her eyes, then snuck a look at Brandon. "I think it's weird and unnatural that we're expected to leap out of bed and attend classes according to some schedule that was just, you know, *imposed* on us. What about our biorhythms?"

"See! You two are totally on the same page. This is why I love Perfect Match so much," Heath said warmly, resting his chin on his hands and practically wriggling in delight, like a golden retriever. "Everyone knows it doesn't lie. It tells you exactly who you're meant to be with."

Brandon tried to ignore Heath's syrupy tone. He knew Heath just wanted to get under his skin.

"Well," Cora said, looking from Heath to Brandon and then back again, "it must mean that you have a certain amount of things in common, based on the questionnaire."

"Yes," Heath said, his shit-eating grin practically taking over his face. "Exactly. *Things in common.* That's the reason I believe that Perfect Match is basically the Waverly fortune-teller. *It knows.*"

Brandon was seriously contemplating throwing his latte into Heath's face. Not that he could be sure that would shut him up. Nothing ever could. Then Cora surprised him by turning in her seat, away from Heath, and looking straight at him, her eyes thoughtful when they met his.

"Are you okay?" she asked. "You look upset."

Brandon stared at her for a moment. "Um, I'm fine," he said, and pretended he didn't hear Heath's snort from across the table. But Cora continued to look at him, and there was something about her expression that seemed . . . interested. Concerned.

"Something's wrong," she declared. "Maybe I can help."

Heath smirked at Brandon from across the table while Brandon considered it. It wasn't like Heath had been any help. Brandon's single attempt to talk about Callie the night before had resulted in Heath blaring Sarah McLachlan from his iPhone and asking if Brandon needed to be held.

Cora, meanwhile, was someone Brandon barely knew. She couldn't possibly have any agenda or any hidden allegiances. She probably had a whole life at Waverly that he knew nothing about. A rich, full life that didn't involve Callie Vernon or Easy

Fucking Walsh. In fact, Cora might be the most perfect person in the world to talk to about this.

"My girlfriend broke up with me," he said, looking into Cora's calm, steady eyes. She frowned.

"Dumped him by e-mail," Heath added, leaning even closer across the table and making a wounded face like that e-mail had hurt him, too. "Before class the other day. Just like that. *Pow.*"

"That's awful," Cora said, her eyes widening. She shifted in her seat, and Brandon noticed, almost absently, that she wore a gold chain bracelet around one delicate wrist.

He blinked. "It is," he said. "I mean, it was."

"Sure," Heath interjected. He sat back and raised his voice slightly, like he wanted the table full of sophomore girls next to them to overhear. "But it could be a lot worse. Like when you were with her the last time, and you walked into the rare books room in the library and found her with Easy Walsh's tongue down her throat. Remember that?" His green eyes were brimming with laughter. "Beginning of sophomore year?"

"Yeah, Heath." Brandon glared at him. "I remember that. Jesus."

"So she's broken up with you before," Cora said matter-of-factly but not unkindly. Brandon had the weirdest sense that she was like some kind of therapist, processing what he said but not judging him.

"It's like . . . she has this addiction to this other guy," Brandon said, the words sort of spilling out of him. "Whenever he's near her, she turns into the kind of person who would do something like cheat on her boyfriend or break up with someone by e-mail, but she's really not like that. She changes around him. Like she thinks that someone being awful to her and treating her like shit is actually some big, romantic thing, and she can't help herself." He shook his head. "But she's so much better than that. She's kind and sweet and funny, and when this guy isn't around, everything is great between us. Like, really great. Perfect."

There was a slight pause as he stopped talking, and he could feel his face get hot. He deliberately avoided looking in Heath's direction. But Cora met his gaze and smiled slightly.

"You really love her, don't you?" she asked quietly.

"No shit, Sherlock," Heath said with a snort. But when Brandon looked at him, he was grinning.

Brandon rolled his eyes. What was the point in denying it? "Yeah," he said. "I do."

Cora nodded. "Okay," she said. "I know exactly what you have to do."

"You have a cure for Easy Walsh?" Heath asked, amused. "I think it might be terminal."

"You know there's this heart scavenger hunt thing going on this week, right?" Cora asked Brandon, ignoring Heath. Brandon stared at her. Scavenger hunt? Was she serious? "All you have to do is collect the most hearts, win the competition, and then prove your love to Callie at the dance."

"Wow," Heath said. He paused for a moment, like he was pondering it. Then he let out a laugh. "That's the gayest thing I've ever heard."

Cora turned to look at Heath. Her eyebrows rose a little bit as she stared him down. Brandon couldn't help being a little impressed.

"No, it's not," she said firmly. "It's romantic."

Heath made a scoffing noise.

Cora rolled her eyes at Heath and looked at Brandon. "What's more romantic than a guy making a grand, kind of goofy, but sweet gesture just to tell you he loves you?" she asked. "If Callie's as romantic as you say she is, she'll love it."

Heath laughed again, but Brandon's mind was racing. He found himself nodding. Callie *was* a total romantic. He could picture it suddenly—presenting her with that Sweet Heart thing, and then declaring his love in front of the whole school. He could practically see the soft look in her eyes. Didn't she cry at almost every chick flick with a sappy ending? This would be exactly like one of those movies. But better, because it would be real.

Brandon stood up suddenly. "Thanks, Cora," he said as he gathered his things. He meant it.

"Sure," she said, looking the slightest bit deflated. Probably because he was leaving her alone with Heath.

As he made his way out of Maxwell, Brandon felt better than he had in the twenty-four hours or so since Callie had sent that e-mail. He wasn't going to sit around and mope anymore.

He was going to win her back.

A WAVERLY OWL KNOWS TO PICK HIS BATTLES.

Easy hadn't planned to bail on his Human Figure Drawing class. He'd packed up his art supplies and headed for the studio in Jameson House with every intention of drawing until his mood improved. He was thinking charcoals and bold lines might come close to expressing his feelings. Definitely an improvement over sitting in his room, staring at the ceiling and wondering what Callie was doing or why she'd dumped him the way she had.

But when he'd made it outside and into the crystal clear, cold afternoon, his body had other ideas. He'd found himself headed out to the stables instead. Maybe it was just the crisp winter air. The sun reflected off the snow and made the icicles on the tree branches glitter like diamonds. Suddenly he had to ride Credo.

He crossed through the woods, taking one of the many shortcuts to the stables that kept him out of sight of academic

buildings that were filled with teachers interested in his where-
abouts. He paused when he spotted a lone figure, moving slowly
in the opposite direction, on the far side of one of the unused
sports fields. Easy stared, perplexed. There was something odd
about the way the other guy was moving.

He realized two things almost simultaneously: (a) the guy
was looking for something on the ground in the field and (b)
the guy was Brandon Buchanan.

Brandon was the last person in the world Easy wanted to
see. Why was the always neatly dressed, always following-the-
rules, always Mr. Perfect Buchanan out so far from the main
campus during a class period? He never came this way. Nobody
really did, unless they were headed to the stables, and Brandon
didn't ride.

Weird, Easy thought, and then, with a last brooding look at
Brandon, he kept going.

He didn't really like to think about Brandon or the fact
that Callie had gotten back together with him—even if she
had dumped him, too. Easy lit a cigarette and blew out a long
plume of smoke into the frigid air. When he was at military
school, he would sneak out of his dorm at night to smoke out
the window of the communal bathroom, the one time all day he
could be alone and think. Usually when he was there he'd think
about Callie, about when they could be together again. Now he
was back, and nothing had changed.

He smoked his cigarette as he walked through the quiet
winter woods. He put his cigarette out when he finally crested
that last hill and saw the stable before him. His refuge. His

boots crunched into the hard crust of snow on the path, and he shoved his cold hands into the pockets of his coat as he walked toward the building.

Inside, the soothing sounds of horses moving in their stalls mixed with the usual hay and horse smells of the stables. Easy felt better immediately. He walked to Credo's stall, smiling when she harrumphed and thrust her nose at him, demanding he pet her. He obliged, patting her wet nose and running a hand down her silky mane. Being here in the stables, with all its sights and smells, brought back the night that Callie had found him here last month. She'd come running out to find him after the party in the middle of the night. He'd thought the fact that she'd come, that she'd known where he was at that very moment, meant something. He'd *wanted* it to mean something.

He moved inside the stall and rubbed his hands down Credo's smooth, warm back. But after a while, it was clear that he was only going to wallow in his Callie problems if he stood around, so he decided he'd better ride instead. A good gallop had never managed to shake Callie Vernon's hold on him, but it always made him feel a little bit better. It cleared his head, at the very least.

He walked back out of the stall, closing the wooden gate behind him and heading for the tack room to get Credo's saddle. The window above let the afternoon sun in, lighting up the hay beneath his feet. His artist's eye couldn't help following the grace-ful beam of sunlight—all the way from the glass, through the air where little dust motes danced, down to the hay scattered on the stable floor. He frowned when he spotted something unusual down in the nearest hay bale, and squatted down to take a closer look. It was a bright red and shiny plastic heart. It even had the Waverly horned-owl emblem stamped onto it.

Valentine's Day, Easy thought, shaking his head as he held the plastic heart in his hand. He had a vague recollection of some e-mail about a scavenger hunt and hearts. But he couldn't remember any details from freshman or sophomore year—he'd probably been drunk at the Valentine's Day dances. He generally tried to be drunk at most dances, as a matter of fact. It was his policy for mandatory social events. Callie had always gotten really pissed about it. *Why can't we have one nice night?* she'd once yelled at him. Easy straightened and almost threw the heart back into the hay.

But then he remembered something else: Brandon Buchanan's unusual presence out in the old field and the fact that he'd clearly been looking for something. Easy knew, in a sudden flash of certainty, that Brandon was looking for these stupid, cheesy hearts.

And he knew exactly why he was doing it.

For Callie.

It was obviously the kind of thing Buchanan, with his pathological need to be the supernaturally perfect boyfriend, would be all over. Easy knew it. And he also knew that Callie would love it. She would eat it up. She might pretend she thought it was dumb, but the truth was, she would melt.

And Easy would be damned if he would sit around moping while Buchanan was the one to make her feel like that.

He stuck the plastic heart in his pocket and felt his own heart beat a little faster. He didn't care if feeling competitive about something so lame probably meant he was lame, too, by definition.

He was going to find every goddamned heart on campus— and win Callie's back in the process.

SebastianValenti: What's up, Red? Where are you???

BrettMesserschmidt: Sorry, did we have plans?

SebastianValenti: It's late afternoon. I know you don't have class and you know I'm in my room. Usually this means you are also in my room. But I've barely seen you all week . . .

BrettMesserschmidt: I'm so sorry. I have this thing to do, but I'll see you at dinner, right?

SebastianValenti: Should I be worried that your "thing" is more interesting than hanging out with me?

BrettMesserschmidt: No! Just this annoying research project I'm working on . . .

SebastianValenti:: I'm very good at research. I'd be happy to show you.

BrettMesserschmidt: Ha! You are too cute. I'll see you later!

SebastianValenti: That's what you said yesterday.

A WAVERLY OWL KNOWS THAT KNOWLEDGE IS POWER.

Brett tossed her phone back on her bed in Dumbarton
121. She glanced over at Tinsley, who was lying across
her own bed with her laptop open before her and a gray
cashmere throw wrapped around her slender body to ward off
the chill.

"Are you ready?" Tinsley asked, impatience threaded
through her voice. She rolled her violet-colored eyes as if
Brett had been holding her up. Brett decided to overlook
her attitude, because she knew Tinsley was just excited and
anxious. So was she. Besides, being involved in this particular "research project" with Tinsley was the closest the two
of them had been in a long time. It made the fact that they
were roommates fun again. Like it had been when they'd lived
together with Callie.

Brett lit the Le Labo vintage candle they kept on the

windowsill in its battered little tin container. It was supposed to smell like St. Barts. Much more soothing than their stuffy dorm room.

"I'm more than ready," Brett said, straightening and tossing the lighter onto the cracked mahogany windowsill next to the candle.

She felt a little bit guilty about not telling Sebastian what she was doing—but this was important. All she had to do was recall the way Isla flirted with Sebastian, and any doubts she might have had disappeared. Isla was perfectly comfortable throwing coy looks at Sebastian when Brett was *sitting right there.* Imagine what the girl got up to when she and Sebastian were somewhere alone!

Brett settled herself on Tinsley's never-made bed. She straightened her Nanette Lepore sweater dress, making sure the batik-patterned sleeves and V-neck sat perfectly, so she would make a good impression. She ran her hands along the smooth sides of her bright red bob as Tinsley pulled up Skype on her computer. The revving sound made Brett's stomach twist a little bit in anticipation.

They'd found Xander Coffey on Facebook late last night, after some trial and error and a totally pervy encounter with some gross thirty-year-old guy from Alexandria, Virginia. But they had no idea what this ex-boyfriend of Isla's was really like. He'd had a picture of Jon Hamm from *Mad Men* as his profile picture, which gave them nothing to go on, really, except that he thought he was smooth.

"What kind of asshole do you think this Xander is going to

be?" Tinsley asked. Brett smiled as she considered. He had to be a total jackass. After all, he'd dated Isla and had practically jumped at the chance to talk about her with two girls he'd never even heard of.

"Oh, you know," Brett said, scrunching up her nose while she thought about it. She kind of thought he'd be a Heath Ferro type, but Tinsley had been remarkably touchy about Heath lately, so she decided not to use him as her example. "Probably one of those over-the-top, obviously hot guys. You know? Definitely not sweet and clean-cut like Brandon or anything. More like Drew Gately. *Too* hot, *too* rich, *too* in love with himself. Blah blah blah." She waved a hand in the air.

"Your basic prep-school douche," Tinsley said happily. She tapped her fingers against the side of her laptop, bouncing slightly on the bed with excitement. "Luckily, we know exactly how to deal with that kind of guy."

"You could say we're experts," Brett agreed, tucking her legs beneath her and concentrating on the screen. "Can you believe they have matching tattoos? And now they're broken up and he has her *name* or something tattooed on his body? Serves him right." She shook her head. "I want to hear about every single threesome and every *hint* of drug use." The plan was to gather dirt on Isla and use it against her when she least expected it.

"Believe me," Tinsley purred, "he'll tell us what we want to know. Guys like Xander live to brag about their exploits, right? All we have to do is pout a little bit." She immediately demonstrated, giving her best sex-kitten look. Tinsley eyed Brett. "You should do that cute little giggling thing you do. He'll love it."

Brett couldn't help herself—she giggled. They looked at each other and burst out laughing.

"Check it out," Tinsley said suddenly, sitting up and expertly tousling her long, black hair so that it tumbled sexily around her shoulders. "Here he comes."

Brett quickly slicked her Creamy Gold Dior Crème de Gloss over her lips and then gazed at the screen expectantly.

Tinsley felt her mouth drop open as the screen filled with the image of a guy about their age. She took in his thick, unfashionable glasses, WHAT THE FRAK? T-shirt, bushy and unkempt red hair, and shy, nervous smile. *This* was Isla's Xander? She'd been expecting Spencer Pratt . . . and she'd gotten Jonah Hill.

"Um, hi," Brett said, when it became clear Tinsley wasn't going to speak. She cleared her throat. "You're Xander Coffey? The one who, um, dated Isla Dresden?"

"That's me," the guy said. His eyes lit up—or maybe that was just the reflection from his thick lenses. "You guys are friends of hers? Isn't she *terrific*?" He said the last word like it was part of a prayer.

Tinsley couldn't look at Brett. This was just too good. Too delicious for words. Isla Dresden, Waverly's resident bad girl, had dated the biggest dork in the world. Things were looking up.

Finally.

"She's an amazing girl," Tinsley drawled, and smiled at Xander like they were BFFs.

"Truly one of a kind," Brett agreed dryly with a smile of her own. Tinsley snuck her hand over to pinch Brett beneath the camera's reach, where Xander couldn't see. Brett's smile got a little bit wider, and Tinsley could tell she was trying hard not to laugh.

"So what can I do for you guys?" Xander asked, his face open and trusting. "You said it was a surprise for Isla? I'll do whatever I can to help."

"That would be great," Tinsley purred. "Here at Waverly we make a really big deal out of Valentine's Day. We have a big slideshow, and everyone submits their favorite pictures of each other. But we realized that Isla's so new that no one has any pictures of her, and we don't want her to feel left out." She batted her lashes for emphasis.

"The slideshow plays at the Valentine's Day Ball," Brett jumped in, keeping her eyes wide and guileless. She pinched Tinsley back beneath the computer. "We really want to make sure Isla feels like she's part of the community here."

"That's a great idea!" Xander said, grinning. "She'll love that." He looked down, and there were sounds of his mouse clicking and tapping against his keyboard. "I have a bunch of photos right here. Where should I send them?"

Tinsley rattled off her e-mail address, and then she and Brett exchanged a long look, laced with excitement. Surely some of Xander's photos with Isla would feature *him*. Nothing could be more priceless than Isla, decked out in her usual skank gear, holding hands with her *Battlestar Galactica*–loving boyfriend.

Tinsley's e-mail beeped, and Xander grinned into the camera. "There you go," he said. "That's only, like, twenty of my favorites. If you need more, feel free to e-mail. I have a ton of other pictures, too."

Tinsley clicked open her e-mail and scrolled through, looking over her shoulder and widening her eyes at Brett. She nearly gasped when she realized what she was staring at. There was a shot of a person only recognizable as Isla thanks to the green eyes. The rest of her was a poufy, frizzy-haired mess, in maryjanes and tapered jeans. There was another shot of Isla and Xander dressed as space cowboys on Halloween. And yet another one of Isla in a victory pose, brandishing a debate-team trophy overhead with a huge smile on her face. Tinsley had to cover her mouth with her hand to keep from shrieking with laughter.

Clearly, Isla's "big secret" was that she'd undergone a massive makeover before coming to Waverly. *She'd die if anyone found out*—if anyone found out that in a past life, she'd moonlighted as a giant nerd. Her bitchy thing was just an act. A clever, well-executed act.

It was actually impressive, Tinsley was forced to admit, however grudgingly, that Isla had taken such upsetting raw material and managed to turn it into such an intriguing, badass package. Even Tinsley had been taken in initially.

But no more.

"Thank you so much," she said, smiling at Xander. "I will

personally make sure that every single one of these makes it into the slideshow."

"Like I said, I'm happy to help," Xander said, his cheeks coloring slightly. "We miss her around here."

"Well," Tinsley said, her smile widening, victory completely and utterly assured, "I can see why."

A WAVERLY OWL IS RELENTLESS IN HER PURSUIT OF THE TRUTH.

Callie paced the floor of her dorm room for approximately the eighteen millionth time. She put her hands on her hips and pivoted, slowly, unsure of what to do with herself. She had already changed her clothes six times. She looked at the piles of discarded outfits that covered the floor in front of her closet and picked at the hem of the ruby L.A.M.B. cardigan she'd finally thrown over a pair of chocolate brown Citizens of Humanity cords, still not satisfied.

But she knew it wasn't the clothes. She hadn't woken up to discover that she suddenly hated her entire wardrobe. It was her skin she couldn't seem to feel comfortable in. Like it was three sizes too small, and she was straining at the seams.

Callie scraped her hair back, piling the blown-out strawberry blond locks on top of her head, and then let it all fall, letting out a heavy sigh.

It had been a day. *An entire day.* More than twenty-four whole hours, and so far absolutely nothing had happened. *Nothing.*

Neither Easy nor Brandon had responded to her e-mail. Neither one of them had texted or called her to discuss what she'd done. Neither of them had showed up at Dumbarton to prove his love to her as anticipated, and she hadn't so much as glimpsed either one of them around campus.

It was like Callie had thrown a giant stone into a pond and the surface of the water hadn't even moved. Like it was blank and still, *mocking* her.

She blinked. She was obviously going insane. She had to get out of her room immediately, before she wrecked her manicure tearing her hair out, or found herself curled in the corner dressed in head to toe black, listening to loud emo music.

Callie swept her camel Michael Kors coat up off the back of her desk chair and left the room before it sucked her in. She ran down the stairs and threw open the heavy emergency door, pushing her way out into the cold evening. It was barely five-thirty, and yet it was already as pitch-black as if it was the dead of night—which actually suited her mood perfectly.

She hunched into her coat and set out across the quad, ducking her head to avoid the students running to study meetings or early dinners, not realizing until she reached the front steps of Richards where she was headed. But then, of course, she knew what she had to do. She marched up to the room Alan shared with Easy and pounded on the door. Maybe Easy would be there. She could at least see him and try to figure out what he was thinking about the whole thing. But she was kind of hoping he wouldn't be there, because she'd much rather see—

"Alan!" she cried when he opened the door. He blinked at her as if the light from the hallway was a blinding searchlight, rather than one dim fluorescent bulb that the guys on the floor habitually broke on purpose.

"Um, hi," he said. "Don't knock like that, Callie. I thought you were a teacher. Jesus. I almost jumped out the window."

"Sorry," she said, more to be polite than anything else. "Please tell me you have more of those brownies. I *need* one!" All she wanted to do right now was laugh herself nearly hoarse and feel *relaxed*.

"Yeah, those are totally gone," Alan said, shaking his head sorrowfully. "The edibles never last long. Want to come in?"

"Sure," Callie said, trying not to feel disappointed. It wasn't like pot brownies were a real solution, anyway. She stepped inside the small dorm room and instantly regretted it. There was too much Easy everywhere. The faint smell of horses, hay, cigarettes, and sweat hung in the incense-scented air. His side of the room was neater than it had been before—another lingering effect of military school, maybe—but there were his old Levi's thrown at the foot of his bed and his art supplies stacked in an efficient if sloppy pile down on the floor beside it. Callie swallowed and then made herself turn and sit in Alan's desk chair as if she couldn't care less.

"Want to smoke or something?" Alan asked. He eyed her for a moment. "You look stressed."

He didn't wait for her answer. He pulled out a joint from

the pocket of his beat-up gray Middlebury Football hoodie and offered it to her.

"No, thanks," Callie said.

"Seriously." Alan's eyebrows rose over his sleepy eyes. "You're, like, twitching."

"It's just that *nothing* has happened!" Callie exclaimed, kind of embarrassed that she was wailing but also not sure she cared. "I mean, I expected *something*. A text message! A *look* from across the dining hall! I don't know. But there hasn't been a single peep out of either one of them!"

Alan stared at her for another moment, and then he ran a hand through his shaggy hair and shook his head. He looked longingly at the unlit joint before shoving it back in his pocket. Without a glance at Callie, he went over to Easy's bed and reached underneath it, pulling out a blue shoebox. Without a word, he took off the lid and presented the box to her, as though the box were on a silver platter.

At first Callie couldn't make sense of what she was seeing. But the red mess eventually separated into plump little plastic hearts, all with owls stamped into their round bellies. Callie reached over and touched one of the hearts, feeling the hard plastic with her fingertips.

That stupid scavenger hunt, the one that made everyone laugh because it was so lame and no one ever did it.

She tried to imagine Easy, of all people, going on a scavenger hunt around the Waverly campus. Collecting hearts.

For her.

She looked up at Alan, a grin breaking across her face, while relief and jubilation soared within her.

"You are a genius!" she cried.

"I don't know about that," Alan said, but he smiled back.

Callie was so excited that she jumped to her feet and then couldn't resist giving Alan a quick little peck on his scruffy cheek.

"I will never be able to thank you," she whispered, happiness surging through her and seeming to bubble beneath her skin.

She let it carry her right back out the door and into the night.

A WAVERLY OWL WILLINGLY ASKS DIFFICULT QUESTIONS.

Jenny waited for Isaac's English seminar to let out from its evening meeting, shifting impatiently from one foot to the other in the brutally overheated foyer of Hunter Hall. She'd carefully dressed in a dark red Anthropologie sweater with ruffled sleeves. If things went poorly, she was counting on her favorite sweater to make her feel a little bit better.

The seminar room door opened, and she took a quick, deep breath. She could do this. She *needed* to do this. It was what normal people did in normal relationships, without all the worrying and wondering and dire warnings from their friends. They needed to just talk.

So why did it feel so hard?

Owls flooded down the steps, complaining loudly that they were hungry and it was too dark, but Jenny only smiled and nodded absently at faces she recognized, like bleached blond Evelyn Dahlie, because she was looking for one face in particular.

Isaac's. He walked out of the seminar room, and when he saw her standing there his face broke into a smile. Immediately some of Jenny's panic eased. His dark hair curled messily, and his pale green eyes contrasted with his tanned skin. She suddenly remembered seeing him for the first time, on the first day of the new term, when she'd been sitting in the chapel and he'd been up on stage behind his dad. He'd caught her eye and smiled at her like he'd known her forever. She felt the same warmth spread through her now.

"Hey," he said, walking over to her. "What are you doing here?"

"I thought I'd surprise you," Jenny replied. She handed him one of the insulated travel mugs she'd been holding in her hands. "I even brought you hot chocolate. It's pretty cold out there." He'd brought them both hot chocolate when they went on their first "date," a winter walk to the crater. She'd been swept away by the sweet gesture, and now she hoped he would be, too.

Isaac's smile deepened, and he moved closer. "How awesome are you?" he asked, taking the mug gratefully. He stepped out of the flow of traffic and joined Jenny in the little alcove by the windows above the stairs.

"I want to ask you something," Jenny blurted out, afraid if she waited she'd lose her nerve.

"Sure," Isaac said easily. He took a sip of his hot chocolate and made an approving noise. He sank down on the top step and patted the space beside him. Jenny sat down on the wide, cold stone, feeling encouraged. Isaac didn't seem nervous. Surely, if he was hiding something, he would be nervous that she wanted to ask him questions, wouldn't he?

She waited until the last student had sailed through the heavy outside doors and then squared her shoulders. "Is there something I should know about?" she asked. She willed herself to look him in the eye.

Isaac frowned, confused. "I don't think so," he said slowly. "Unless you want me to tell you about Virginia Woolf. We just talked about her in class. But you've probably read *A Room of One's Own*, right?"

Jenny bit her lip to keep from smiling and plowed on. "It's just that you were really weird earlier this week," she said quickly. Maybe if they got this over with, they really *could* talk about Virginia Woolf or something else entirely. "You usually walk me all the way to Dumbarton, but the minute I started talking about Valentine's Day, you took off. Was something going on?"

Their eyes met. Jenny panicked. What if he wasn't going to answer? What if he *was* going to answer and it was something bad? But then Isaac blinked.

"Oh my God," he said, shaking his head. "I am so sorry." His green eyes were serious when they met hers. "Of course you thought something was up." He sighed. "What was up was that I completely forgot it was Valentine's Day. I had some things that I had to take care of. But now it's done, and I can focus all my energy on you."

Jenny imagined the ball again, with Isaac looking at her exactly the way he was now, so serious and earnest, dipping her over his arm, then spinning her around and around. . . .

"Okay," she said softly. "I just wondered."

"I had this cute girl wanting me to be romantic so of course I froze," Isaac said gently, moving closer to her on the step. "I was wondering how I could possibly have forgotten. I mean, Valentine's Day requires some preparation, Jenny."

"It does?" Jenny asked, but she could feel a goofy grin taking over her face. She couldn't believe that she'd been so worried about this for so long, and he'd just been dealing with something else entirely. And he'd called her *cute*.

"Of course," Isaac said. He handed her back the mug she'd given him and dug around in his bag. He pulled out a thin, flat box and suddenly looked almost shy.

"I wanted you to have this," he said. Jenny's hands were full, so he opened the box and pulled out a small, framed sketch. Jenny recognized it immediately. One afternoon during Jan Plan, she and Isaac had been sitting in Maxwell while Jenny sketched, and she had sketched their hands as they'd both held on to a single cappuccino mug. It had just been a silly doodle.

"That's the first picture you ever drew of us," Isaac said. His mouth curved. "I thought it should be framed."

Something warm started to glow inside of her, heating her up from the inside out. "I think you're kind of amazing," Jenny said, smiling up at him.

"I'm glad you think so," Isaac said. He looked down and then met her gaze again. "Because I'm hoping you'll go to the

Valentine's Day Ball with me. I mean, I know we're supposed to go with our Perfect Matches and everything, but I'm sure Brett will be busy with Sebastian. . . ."

Jenny's heart felt too big for her chest. It was really happening. She could almost *see* the two of them dancing, Isaac's strong arms tight around her, his face pressed close to hers, as her dress swished and swayed to the music. . . .

"Yes," she whispered dreamily. "I'd love to." She thought she might overflow with happiness. Thank God she'd asked Isaac what was happening instead of continuing to stress. Julian's advice was spot-on.

She felt an odd twinge then, thinking of Julian, but she forgot it almost immediately when Isaac moved closer and slid his arm around her shoulders. She tilted her head back to look at him, her heart fluttering wildly as he leaned over and then pressed his lips to hers.

Jenny felt her toes curl in her carefully chosen Frye boots.

Everything was absolutely and perfectly okay.

BennyCunningham: Are you excited for your romantic date with Drew??

SageFrancis: Do you think anyone would notice if I bailed? There must be other guys who need dates. . . .

BennyCunningham: Keep your grubby paws off my Perfect Match!

SageFrancis: Um, hello, been there and done that. He's all yours.

AlisonQuentin: Is it weird that I'm acting like the ball is, like, the prom?

CelineColista: Hell no! If I was going with Parker DuBois, I'd be giving it the full Cinderella treatment too.

AlisonQuentin: He is so hot. . . . I can't stand it.

CelineColista: If you really can't stand it, I'm sure I can. Feel free to share.

AlisonQuentin: Over my dead body.

AlanStGirard: I hate dressing up. I hate dancing. This is like torture.

RyanReynolds: Yeah, but girls love it.

AlanStGirard: I don't think Kara loves it. Or you.

RyanReynolds: Dude. I have to take her, but that doesn't mean I have to leave with her.

BennyCarmichael: I certainly hope you collected all those plastic hearts for me. ;)

LonBaruzza: Does anyone actually do that?

BennyCarmichael: Only if they're pathetic. Or twelve. Make sure you bring refreshments.

LonBaruzza: You know it.

A WAVERLY OWL FACES UP TO THE CONSEQUENCES
OF HER ACTIONS.

Callie nervously smoothed her hands along the ruched sides of her formfitting, scarlet Zac Posen dress, shifting her weight from one hot pink Kate Spade slingback to the other. She'd spent hours perfecting her casual yet sophisticated side-swept ponytail, and she knew her hair looked terrific. Even Alan, currently standing next to her and zoning out on one of the slowly spinning disco balls suspended from the ceiling, had managed to focus long enough to tell her she looked pretty.

Now if only Easy would show up, everything would be the way it was supposed to be. Callie bit her lip as her eyes scanned the Owls crowding into the transformed Reynolds Atrium. It was a two-story space courtesy of a hefty donation from Ryan Reynolds's contact-lens-king father, complete with a glass barrel-vaulted ceiling designed by I. M. Pei. The Valentine's Day Ball committee had done an incredible job. The space shone with red and gold and pink and silver—from the helium balloons in V-Day colors to the gentle pink lights that made the room feel more intimate than it was. The usual red Pottery Barn couches blended right in, and the green-and-gold paisley carpet was covered by a temporary dance floor. Even Callie, who was admittedly jaded about some things, thought the room looked gorgeous.

She adjusted the bright red strap on her shoulder and smiled automatically at the familiar faces that streamed by her, as all the Perfect Match couples wandered into the ball in varying states of awkwardness. Tinsley and Brett marched in arm in arm, whispering to each other, while Heath and Sebastian trailed behind, sharing sips from Heath's trusty flask. Jenny, wearing one of Callie's dresses, was making googly eyes at Isaac, despite the fact that he was technically Brett's date. On her other side, Julian McCafferty walked quietly with a resigned look on his face. Rifat Jones was leaning so far into Teague Williams's side, laughing and whispering in his ear, that it was hard to see where her Betsey Johnson dress ended and his Hugo Boss suit began. But Callie couldn't even giggle at the way Kara Whalen and Ryan Reynolds marched in, side by side, looking like they were headed toward a firing squad. She could only really concentrate on peering around Alan's shoulder and wondering why she couldn't spot Easy in the crowd.

She couldn't wait. Adrenaline and excitement coursed through her, leaving her breathless. If she closed her eyes, she could see the whole night spin out perfectly in her mind. Easy would arrive, wearing an impeccably tailored suit despite the fact he detested dressing up. He'd be looking so good, she'd feel fluttery. He would stride across the floor—or maybe gallop across it, astride Credo like some white knight—and present a huge box of hearts to Mrs. Pritchard, who would then present him with the Sweet Heart. Easy would then declare to the entire school that he was in love with Callie and would sweep her into his arms for a romantic dance in the center of the atrium, wedding-style, while everyone cheered and wept. It would all end, of course, in a happily-ever-after kiss. Her heart skipped a few beats as she pictured it.

Mrs. Pritchard appeared then, climbing up onto the little mini-stage they'd constructed beneath the huge, blank white wall where they would be playing the "Love at Waverly" slide-show later. It occurred to Callie that she hadn't bothered to send in any pictures this year, but she forgot it almost immediately as Mrs. Pritchard began talking.

"Your attention please, Owls!" she called into the microphone over the excited buzz of Waverly students decked out in their Valentine's Day Ball best.

In front of Callie, Benny Cunningham took a big swig from Lon Baruzza's flask and then giggled while Lon secured it on the inside of his sleek dark suit jacket. Benny's long brown hair looked pink from the Valentine's Day lighting scheme. Sage Francis stood on Benny's other side, her back stiff and her attention riveted on the stage— presumably so that she wouldn't have to pay any attention to her date, good-looking but incredibly jerky Drew Gately. He was standing so close, Callie had a feeling he was trying to make a move.

"Tonight we celebrate love," Mrs. Pritchard said, and the students immediately groaned and applauded in equal measure. Sage and Benny rolled their eyes at each other. Ryan Reynolds whispered something to Kara that made her smack him on his arm. Hard.

"Come on . . ." Callie muttered under her breath. She shook her head when Alan offered her a drink from the Nalgene bottle he held in his hand. She had to stay focused. This was the moment she'd been waiting for.

"Let's start with our scavenger hunt," Mrs. Pritchard said.

"Boring!" a group of senior boys shouted in unison. Other kids laughed appreciatively.

"Why don't our contenders bring up their hearts, and we'll start counting them, with or without the unnecessary commentary from the peanut gallery?" Mrs. Pritchard continued brightly, smiling out at the crowd. "Who will be the Waverly Sweet Heart winner this year? Can you stand the suspense?"

For a moment, no one moved, though everyone started talking.

"Is there anything lamer?" Sage asked with a sniff that made her almost white-blond hair bounce. In front of her, Emily Jenkins turned around, shaking her head in agreement.

"Who would want to make such a big spectacle of themselves in front of the whole school?" she asked. "Can you imagine?"

Callie could imagine. She was about to scream in anticipation when there was a ripple in the crowd. Easy was making his way toward the stage, holding his shoebox of hearts. His lean, muscled form was stunningly packaged in the Armani suit of her dreams—something that would have looked laughably out of place on the old, pre-military school Easy. It fit *this* version of Easy Walsh like a glove. Callie felt her heart swell. She could almost feel his kiss on her lips . . . and she closed her eyes for a moment as she imagined it.

But when she opened them, she saw another figure moving toward the stage from the other side of the atrium. *Brandon.* Also in a sleek suit, and also holding a box.

As both guys reached the stage, they looked at each other for a moment. No one else came forward with any hearts. No one else moved. Then, as if on cue, Easy and Brandon turned to find Callie in the crowd. There was a rustling sound, as everyone turned, too. A slight murmur ran through the throng. It was like she was suddenly thrust into a spotlight. Callie summoned up a weak smile.

"Of course," Benny said, loud enough so Callie could hear, her voice dripping with annoyance. "Once a love triangle, always a love triangle. God, it's so fucking boring."

Suddenly Callie had no interest in the hearts or the Sweet Heart dance. She just wanted it to be over. She didn't want to have to choose between the two of them again. She didn't even want them to fight each other. Maybe she'd been right to break it off with both of them—to stop the madness. All of a sudden, more than anything, she just wanted peace.

But instead, they were counting hearts.

Brandon gripped his box between his hands and tried not to look at the very similar box Easy was holding three feet away from him on Mrs. Pritchard's other side. He couldn't believe it. Once again, Easy Fucking Walsh appeared out of nowhere and ruined everything. Like it was his mission on this earth to ruin Brandon's life.

Music blared from the speakers, and the assembled Owls went back to talking and giggling among themselves. Mrs. Pritchard ushered the two of them to the side of the stage, where they had to hand their boxes over to gratingly perky underclassmen seated at a makeshift table . . . and then stand there, waiting. Brandon and Easy. Alone. While the rest of the school watched and waited, too.

They stared at each other. Easy had cleaned up for the event. He'd actually, finally made an effort. Brandon couldn't find a single splatter of paint on his Armani, and with his hair so short and neat, Easy looked like much less of a degenerate than usual.

Great, Brandon thought.

They stood stiffly next to each other while the two freshman volunteers sat at the little table and counted out their collection of hearts. One by one. And with far too much sighing about *how romantic* the whole thing was.

"So much for my great idea," Brandon said. He couldn't help himself at this point, after spending days combing through the most absurd places on campus, thinking he was making this huge, romantic gesture for Callie that no one else—especially not Easy—would ever think to make. Seriously, who even did the scavenger hunt? In the history of Waverly? "Was there, like, an e-mail? *Collect hearts for Callie?*"

Easy eyed him. Buchanan looked miserable, and Easy knew it was his fault. Just like he had many times before, Easy felt guilty. It wasn't Brandon's fault that he was in love with Callie. Of all the people in the world, Easy should probably be the most sympathetic to that particular problem.

"I saw you," he said, admitting it, because it felt like the right thing to do. He owed it to the guy to at least be honest about it. "Out by the stables. And I don't know, I had to do it, too."

Brandon ran his tongue over his teeth. Of course. Of course Easy had copied him. It didn't even bother him, necessarily. It was just more of the same. "So you were competing with me, but you didn't bother to tell me that or anything," he said, frowning. "Nice. I wonder why this feels kind of familiar?"

Easy shrugged uncomfortably. "I know," he said. "I should have told you." Maybe it was because he'd seen Brandon's pile of hearts, and he was pretty sure his was bigger. Maybe that was why he was feeling like he and Brandon should be better friends—or something. Like history shouldn't matter so much. But maybe that was easier when you were the person who usually won.

"Well, why start now?" Brandon said, but his voice was more wry than bitter, and he actually smiled slightly. It was like the absurdity of the whole thing hit them both at the same time.

"Did you go on any of the roofs?" Easy asked with a sideways look. "I saw a couple of hearts out on top of Richards, but no way was I going out there and getting harpooned by an icicle."

"Yeah, no way," Brandon agreed. "It was cold enough on solid ground." He shook his head. He didn't know why he was suddenly so comfortable talking to his nemesis, without even the usual urge to punch the guy in the face. "I guess after being dumped in a three-line e-mail, I'm not really accountable for my actions."

There was a small, charged silence.

"Callie dumped you in an e-mail?" Easy asked, his expression suddenly intense.

Brandon fervently wished he hadn't said anything. "Um, yeah," he said. He could feel his ears heat up. Why had he brought that up, of all things? To Easy, of all people?

"That's funny," Easy said. He turned so he was looking straight at Brandon, his blue eyes suddenly serious. "Me too."

Brandon felt his mouth fall open.

"And the even funnier part?" Easy's head tilted slightly, like he was considering how not funny the whole thing actually was. "My e-mail was three lines long, too, now that I think about it."

"Huh," Brandon said, his mind racing. So if Callie had called things off with Easy, did that mean they *had* been seeing each other behind his back? He knew he should be pissed, and try to find out exactly what Easy meant, but he sort of felt like it didn't even really matter anymore.

"When did you get yours?" Easy asked.

"Wednesday morning," Brandon said. Easy gave a quick, curt nod. Brandon laughed in disbelief. "No fucking way."

"I'm really sorry to do this over e-mail," Easy quoted, his gaze challenging.

Brandon's head was spinning, but he knew that goddamned e-mail by heart. *"I just don't think it's going to work,"* he replied, his stomach tensing. How could she have done something like this?

"*I'm sorry*," they chorused, staring at each other in disbelief.

"So . . ." Brandon shook his head. Even for Callie, who could take being callous to practically an Olympic level, this seemed beyond fucked up. "I can't believe she sent a *form letter*!"

"She played us," Easy said, looking furious.

"And we have a winner!" one of the freshmen cried, jumping up from behind the counting table.

"Save it," Brandon told her. "No one cares."

Together, they turned around and looked at Callie once again. Beautiful, treacherous, two-timing Callie.

Callie did not need to be psychic to interpret the nasty looks that both Brandon and Easy threw at her. Without another glance in her direction, Easy turned and headed for the door. Brandon looked at her as if she'd ripped his heart out—a look she was familiar with—and then stormed off in the opposite direction.

Callie's stomach heaved, and her hand crept over her mouth. Maybe she would throw up on her own shoes. Wouldn't that be just the icing on the whole fucked-up cake?

"Uh-oh," Benny singsonged. "Trouble! Looks like someone's not the Sweet Heart after all!"

Callie ignored her and turned to Alan. He was staring at the helium balloons above them as they danced in the pink light.

"Alan!" she hissed at him. "What happened? They were supposed to fight for me!"

"That sucks," he said, not really focusing on her.

"*That sucks?*" she repeated. "It was *your* idea!"

Alan managed to glance at her then. But he didn't seem at all apologetic. He looked the way he always did: rumpled and stoned.

"Sorry, dude," he said. "I was totally baked when I came up with that whole thing. Want to smoke?"

Callie fought back tears. What had she expected? Why had she listened to the biggest stoner at Waverly in the first place? She felt her stomach twist again and a prickle behind her eyes that let her know she was seconds away from an unstoppable torrent of tears. She shook her head at Alan mutely and then whirled around. She headed blindly for whatever door she could find, to put as much space as possible between herself and this night.

A WAVERLY OWL KNOWS THAT EVEN THE BEST-LAID
PLANS OFTEN GO AWRY.

The lights dimmed in the atrium, and a bright light flickered on the far, blank wall. Everyone quieted down and turned to watch as an ancient picture of Waverly's chapel appeared onscreen with the words LOVE AT WAVERLY written over it in flowing calligraphy. The picture started to fade, and then the intro to the Black Eyed Peas' "I Gotta Feeling" began to play. Everyone clapped and whistled.

The first photo was a pair of horned owls, the Waverly mascots, looking sweet and cuddly. The grim reality was that they were vicious and shit everywhere and weren't opposed to injuring any Waverly students who didn't outrun them. But that was what made them the perfect Waverly mascots, after all. Everyone cheered.

The photos started coming faster as the song picked up. There was one of Callie and co-captain Celine Colista in field hockey gear, arms slung around each other after a match. There was a shot of a party in the Richards lounge. Callie, Brett, Sage, and Benny all sat on a couch, leaning in together and whispering about something. In the next shot, Jenny stood in front of Heath, holding an insulated coffee mug in her hands and smiling up at him. Then, in a bit of editing genius, the very next shot was of Jenny again, performing her famous Heath-bashing cheer from Black Saturday back in September, with the whole field hockey team standing behind her.

While everyone catcalled, Heath took a bow, milking the moment. "Always available, ladies!" he called out.

There were montages of seniors at their convocation in the fall, working on their senior projects and all assembled together in front of Maxwell for their traditional class picture. There were shots of all the sports teams and all the extracurricular teams and clubs. The Waverly paper editorial board. The academic clubs.

There were pictures of freshmen performing silly calisthenics as part of their orientation week. Shots of the Drama Club performing in the black-box theater. And photos of Owls just hanging out, up to their usual forms of mischief. Easy and Jenny with their desks facing each other in art class, drawing on big sketchpads. All the Dumbarton girls in pajamas and sweats, eating bagels and drinking orange juice in the dorm's common room. Alan St. Girard, Ryan Reynolds, Brandon, Heath, and Julian McCafferty, all kicked back at one of the dining hall tables in front of the fireplace. Tinsley and Julian sitting out on one of the stone benches in the quad, Tinsley's legs propped up across his lap. Skinny, birdlike Yvonne Stidder and Kara Whalen in the foyer of Dumbarton, holding stacks of textbooks and making silly faces.

There was what looked like a surveillance shot of Kara Whalen lying on her bed, reading a book, with Brett sitting on the floor next to her, frowning at her MacBook. Another one of Callie and Easy standing close together in a hallway, oblivious to the world around them. Two freshmen girls, elbows linked, smiling secretively. A big group shot of the Women of Waverly—plus Heath—all piled on the red couches in the atrium, cheering at the camera. Owls stretched out on blankets and sitting on bales of hay at the Cinephiles screening in front of the Miller Barn—while it was still standing, obviously taken before the barn burned down that same evening. A couple kissing on the steps outside the biology building. A self-portrait of Kara, Heath, and Brett, their faces all smushed together. Brandon, senior Brian Atherton, and Julian all sweaty and brandishing squash rackets on one of the squash courts.

There was a shot of Brandon and Callie sitting next to each other at a table in Maxwell, laughing like best friends. A flock of underclass girls wearing tank tops, sprawled out on a maroon Waverly blanket on the lawn in front of one of the dorms, trying to soak up some late autumn sun before the upstate New York winter hit. A blurry photo of unidentifiable Owls wearing red, orange, and yellow hanging out at the Crater, a bonfire in front of them and Heath Ferro's heated tents behind them at the Goodbye Us party in the fall. People cheered when that one went up—thankful that no one could get in trouble so far after the fact, because the shot was way too out of focus.

There was an action shot of Celine Colista, Emmy Rosenblum, Verena Arvenal, and Rifat Jones out jogging in the rain, wearing matching maroon Waverly windbreakers over tiny nylon shorts. Heath and Kara on top of the old Waverly Observatory, their legs dangling off the edge of the tower. Jenny dressed in her Halloween contest-winning Cleopatra outfit, next to a grinning Brett dressed as Daphne from *Scooby-Doo!* Heath, Ryan Reynolds, Lon Baruzza, Erik Olssen, Lance Van Brachel, and Alan St. Girard playing basketball in the Field House. The short-lived Men of Waverly club posing together in the Field House—complete with the usually nonathletic Easy and the old dean, Dean Marymount, who was resoundingly booed. And one of Tinsley, Brett, Callie, and Jenny, dancing in their fancy dresses on a table in Cambridge House, looking like they were in love with one another and the whole wide world.

Tinsley remembered how good that dance had felt, but she was on pins and needles tonight. How many schmaltzy pictures was she going to have to look at before they got to the good stuff?

"Maybe they didn't include the photos we sent," Brett whispered nervously from beside her.

They had both ditched their dates once the lights went down, determined to get into the best possible position for Isla's long overdue unmasking. Brett's bright red hair shone in the darkness, and her porcelain skin looked luminous in an ice blue one-shoulder David Meister dress that swept from one jeweled shoulder to just above her knees. She stood out amid all the pinks and reds. Tinsley had opted for maximum attention-getting herself, in a silk Nicole Miller multicolored floor-length dress that tucked in beneath her chest and then floated around her long legs. She'd piled her hair on the top of her head and had worn minimal makeup and accessories, knowing that she looked effortlessly cool and elegant—a startling contrast, she anticipated, to Isla's true, dorked-out face. She could hardly wait for the inevitable comparisons to begin.

"Trust me," she assured Brett. "The pictures are in. The so-called slideshow committee is two sophomore girls who practically peed themselves when I walked into their room. They would have jumped out their window if I'd wanted them to."

"Fear is good," Brett said with a happy sigh.

And then it started. The first shot was one of Tinsley's personal favorites: It featured Isla with her masses of hair clearly untouched by any hint of product and frizzed out around her like a halo, glasses perched on her nose, her face scrunched up as she stared down at a chemistry textbook. The next was Isla in dorky pigtails and a Jonas Brothers concert T-shirt, clearly performing some kind of spastic dance, complete with a hairbrush clutched in her hand as a microphone. There was one of Isla and Xander, cuddled up on the couch with junk food littered all around them, ferociously concentrating on the video games they were playing. Another one of the happy couple featured Xander in some kind of Harry Potter rip-off wizard costume, with Isla sporting fairy wings and a tutu. Then came the food series: Isla chewing something with her mouth wide open, Isla with a straw up her nose, Isla cramming brownies into her face.

God, it was so beautiful. As victory surged through her, Tinsley couldn't help but laugh. She'd seen Isla earlier, looking sleek and mysterious as ever, gliding around the party in a short, black Narciso Rodriguez dress. *Not so pretty now, are you, sweetie?*

Next to Tinsley, Brett waited for triumph to wash over her, but instead, with every shot of Isla in her geekitude, she felt something heavy and cold grow in her stomach. She sucked her bottom lip between her teeth and then sneaked a look over to where Sebastian was leaning against one of the couches to watch the show. She could see the frown on his face and the way his mouth pulled down in the corners. And suddenly she knew what the heaviness inside her was: guilt.

"I have to go," she whispered, but Tinsley didn't hear her—she was too busy cackling with glee as the unflattering pictures of Isla kept rolling. Brett headed for Sebastian and didn't look back.

The lights finally rose as the credits began to play—like anyone cared who the slideshow committee was—and Tinsley was still snickering. It took a few moments of blinking in the pink lights to realize that she was the only one laughing. All around her, people were murmuring to one another and turning to *glare* at Tinsley once they realized she was the one laughing— and therefore, obviously, the one behind the Isla retrospective.

"Geeks rule!" someone shouted. Someone else picked up the cheer.

They have got *to be kidding,* Tinsley thought in disbelief. She turned her head to check out Heath's reaction, but he was already moving toward Isla.

"You still have that fairy costume?" he asked in his usual lascivious way, which could be heard in every corner of the atrium. "What about that tutu?"

Tinsley didn't understand the hot jealousy that jolted through her as Heath's golden brown head tilted close to Isla's dark curls. She wanted to scream something that would force him to turn around, to *see* her. She couldn't believe how much she wanted him to be paying attention to her instead of Isla. But the cold reality sunk in around her, utterly and completely undeniable.

She'd lost.

Again.

Brett followed Sebastian as he walked away from the ball and deeper into ficus and fern territory. When he finally stopped walking—*stomping*, really—Brett felt like they were standing in a jungle. She glanced over her shoulder toward the lights and the crowd, wondering if anyone could see them hidden in this corner.

But then Sebastian turned to look at her, his dark eyes so cold, and she forgot all about the greenery and the party.

"I know you did that," he said, his voice hard. He looked so handsome in his sleek, dark suit that all Brett wanted to do was go back in time, cancel the slideshow, and spend the night dancing with him. "What did you do? Stalk the poor girl? What did she ever do to you?"

"Lucky Isla," Brett threw at him, jealousy clawing at her once again, "that you're so quick to jump to her defense no matter what she does!"

Sebastian looked at her for an uncomfortably long moment, his expression remote. Tired. Suddenly the jealousy that had burned so intensely inside her seemed to sputter out. It was replaced by something new—something worse. Fear.

"I can't believe this," he said, raking his fingers through his thick, dark hair. He hadn't put any gel in it—Brett was always begging him to go product-free—and this was the first time all night she'd noticed. "This is more of your jealous bullshit, isn't it?"

"She hangs all over you!" Brett protested, but her voice sounded weak even to her own ears.

"For the record," Sebastian snapped, "I didn't wake up one day and think it would be cool to hang out with the girl. It was a Perfect Match thing. Aren't you matched up with her brother? Do you see me freaking out? Even though, let's face it, you have been acting shifty and weird lately."

Brett had to look away from him then, because she didn't know what to say and she was afraid she might burst into tears.

"But it doesn't matter, does it?" Sebastian's voice was bitter. "You're so fucking insecure that you plotted to embarrass her, just because I was *nice* to her."

"No . . ." Brett protested, but there was no force behind the word. She felt almost frozen. She couldn't seem to do anything but look at Sebastian's disappointed face while he stared down at her.

"I can't keep doing this," he said, the ring of finality in his voice. Brett's heart kicked in her chest, and her stomach dropped to her knees, but she still couldn't seem to speak. "I can't be with you if you're going to act like this all the time. What's next? Are you going to go after my lab partner because we share the same table? I just . . . I can't take it anymore."

He didn't give Brett a chance to defend herself or to explain. He just brushed past her and walked away.

26

A WAVERLY OWL KNOWS THAT THE TRUTH WILL SET HER FREE—IF IT DOESN'T KILL HER FIRST.

Jenny sat with Isaac on one of the red couches that had been pushed back from the main crowd in the atrium. The slideshow had left a bad taste in Isaac's mouth, he'd said, and he'd drawn Jenny away with him. She was happy to go. The whole Isla montage was weird and regrettable, but it hadn't made a dent in Jenny's good mood. Isaac had been so sweet and romantic all night. Everyone had gone to the ball with their Perfect Matches, but even though he was technically Brett's date, he'd made it clear he was with Jenny from the moment they got to the ball, handing her one red rose. Julian had taken one look at the two of them, given Isaac that boy-head nod of acknowledgment, and left to go hang out with his buddies. Now Jenny was twirling the rose between her fingers, waiting for the one thing she'd wanted all along: a Valentine's Day kiss.

"Poor Isla," Isaac said, shaking his head. Jenny reached over and put her hand on his, and he smiled at her, warming her up from the inside out until she was sure she must have matched the pink blush of the Marc Jacobs dress she'd borrowed from Callie's closet.

"She's changed so much," Jenny ventured to say. She knew what it felt like to be on the receiving end of Tinsley's hatred, so she couldn't help but feel a little sorry for Isla. Then again, Isla wasn't exactly angelic. She'd lied to get Tinsley in trouble.

But this was Isla's brother, after all. Hardly an impartial observer.

"She was obsessed with it," Isaac said, leaning back against the red couch. "The minute Dad got the new job, she decided that she was going to completely reinvent herself. She was, like, on a mission."

Jenny felt a reluctant stirring inside, knowing that she, of all people, could relate to that idea. But then a memory tickled at her, and she frowned. "Wait," she said. "I thought you told me that you had to leave your old school because Isla did something bad . . . ?"

Isaac sighed. "If you mean she maxed out a credit card buying ridiculous clothes in New York City." He shrugged. "When we first got here, she kind of wanted to let people think that she was trouble, you know? So . . . I sort of helped. In reality, she's a good girl. We really just moved here for my dad's career."

"I guess it's nice that you helped her out," Jenny said. She smiled at him. "But I'm glad you're telling me the truth now."

She felt as if a little glow surrounded them. They really were a real couple, because he was telling her the truth about things. Jenny decided she was proud of them both.

"I'm sorry I lied about it," he said. He turned slightly so he was facing her, his green eyes serious and his mouth curved into an adorable smile. His dark jacket hung open over his crisp white shirt. "It just . . . it was so important to her."

Jenny's heart melted. Isaac was such a good guy. He took care of his sister. He'd looked worried sick during the slideshow.

"I understand," she said. "Family has to come first." She thought of her brother, Dan, and how worried he got about her sometimes. He would have freaked out if someone had put on a slideshow just to humiliate her. And it wouldn't have been hard to do, given how much trouble she'd gotten herself into back at Constance Billard and even here at Waverly.

"My older brother is totally overprotective," she said, taking Isaac's hand between hers. She shrugged, smiling. "That's his job."

Isaac's lips moved into a grin and his hand tightened on hers. "I guess I just think I should have taken better care of her."

"I'm sure she knows that," Jenny assured him. "Little sisters always know that their brothers are looking out for them."

Isaac's smile deepened. Jenny felt the rose between her fingertips, happy that there were no secrets between them now. She leaned closer into him. A remote couch in a semi-dark corner wasn't just a great place for sharing secrets—it would also be a great place for a kiss. She hadn't been able to get their last kiss, in the English building the other day, out of her head. She swayed closer. Isaac's mouth curved, and he leaned toward her.

"Isaac?"

Jenny blinked and turned toward the voice. A girl stood a few feet away from the couch, frowning ferociously. Talk about throwing cold water on a moment. Jenny wondered what the unfamiliar girl wanted and pasted a polite smile on her face. But next to her, Isaac went rigid, threw Jenny's hand off his, and jumped to his feet.

"Molly!" he cried in a voice Jenny barely recognized. Did he sound . . . nervous?

She stood up, too, frowning at the girl. Molly was slender with chocolate brown hair to her shoulders and bright, quizzical brown eyes. She wore jeans and an emerald green sweater with a puffy black parka unzipped and hanging open and a thermos in her hands. She looked from Isaac to Jenny and then back again, her brows knitted in confusion.

"What are you doing here?" Isaac asked, stepping closer to the other girl and farther away from Jenny. A shiver went down her spine, but she ignored it.

"I couldn't not see you on Valentine's Day," Molly said. Her worried brown eyes shifted to Jenny, who felt more and more exposed and uncomfortable the longer the moment dragged out. The girl's eyes flicked back to Isaac. "I know you hate being sick, so I brought you some of your favorite chicken soup." She indicated the thermos she clutched between her hands. "But you're . . . um . . . all dressed up. At a dance."

She didn't say *with this girl*, but Jenny was pretty sure they all heard it anyway.

"Isaac," Jenny said, choking a little bit on his name, "what's going on?"

She knew. She just didn't *want* to know. She didn't want to believe it—but it was literally standing right in front of her. It was the way the other girl was looking at him, the expectation and confusion and hurt in her brown eyes. Jenny could think of only one reason a girl would show up at a ball, dressed so casually, bearing chicken soup for a guy who wasn't even sick.

Her stomach hurt.

"Um, this is Jenny . . ." Isaac said, gesturing toward Jenny. His words trailed off.

"I'm Molly," the other girl said, cocking her head slightly as she looked at Jenny. Her eyes traveled over Jenny's curls, her large chest, down the sleek front of her dress to her shoes and right back up again. Her gaze darkened. Jenny knew what she was going to say next in the same way she knew that the sun was going to come up in the morning. "Isaac's girlfriend."

"You have a girlfriend." Jenny couldn't get the words to make sense. She felt tears threaten her eyes. "I can't believe you!" She could hardly breathe. "Is this the 'thing you had to take care of'? Which you obviously *didn't*. It was a total lie."

"And you're definitely not sick, Isaac," Molly said, her voice sharpening. "You told me you thought you were dying. You said you were stuck in bed and probably would be for the rest of the week, and that's why you couldn't come visit!"

"No, no," Isaac said hurriedly. "Wait, you don't under-stand!"

Jenny took a step away from him and suddenly everything made a horrible kind of sense. Isaac's noticeable weirdness when she'd mentioned the Valentine's Day Ball in the first place. Had he been worried about his girlfriend then? When had he told Molly he wasn't going to go see her? She was willing to bet it was right around the time he started acting normal, sweet, and attentive again.

Jenny shut her eyes for a moment, afraid the room might start spinning in time with her head. Why was she so con-sistently, repeatedly wrong about guys? Epically, tragically wrong?

"I didn't want to tell you I was feeling better," Isaac was tell-ing Molly. "I didn't think I could drive all the way there. . . ."

He was still lying. Was there anything he *hadn't* lied about? Jenny backed away from the two of them, her stomach twist-ing, tears pricking the backs of her eyes. How could she be so blind, over and over again? So completely clueless?

Her eyes scanned the party, desperate to find a shoulder to cry on. Her gaze landed on Brett's distinctive hair in the crowd. Brett was standing almost inside the plants near the windows, all alone. They met each other's gaze across the sea of pink-lit ferns. She started to move toward her friend.

But then something occurred to her. Brett's strange reaction to Jenny's use of the word *boyfriend*. Her deflating words at the Three-Legged Race. She'd seemed so wary, even concerned . . . almost as if she'd known the truth about Isaac.

It hit Jenny like a tidal wave: she'd known. There was no *almost* about it. Her supposed friend had known Isaac was two-timing her, and she'd lied right to Jenny's face.

Which meant that Jenny hadn't just lost a boyfriend—she'd lost a friend. Isaac was a liar, but maybe her entire life at Waverly was a lie, too.

She glared at Brett and then ran away before all the liars and cheaters and backstabbers could see her cry.

27

A WAVERLY OWL KNOWS EXACTLY WHO HER FRIENDS ARE.

Tinsley didn't exactly *retreat* into the bathroom. She wasn't one for slinking off. But she couldn't deny that when she did go to the bathroom, at an unhurried pace that would not have looked out of place on a catwalk, it was a relief to get a break from the collective evil eye that was trained on her.

Oh, well. *All publicity is good publicity,* her father always said. Better that everyone should be talking about her than failing to notice her, she told herself, and she tried to make herself believe it. She really did.

She looked at herself in the mirror as she washed her hands. Truth be told, she would rather be adored, but she'd make do with what she had. *Not like you have much choice,* an inner voice whispered. Tinsley slapped off the faucet and reached for a paper towel.

A stall door opened behind her, and Isla walked out. For a moment, they just stared at each other through the bank of mirrors.

Isla recovered first. She raised her brows and walked toward Tinsley, stopping at the next sink over.

"I guess we're even," she said, but she didn't sound triumphant. She sounded resigned.

Tinsley smiled wanly. Were they even? Isla had sold Tinsley out, consigned her to a month of hard labor, and then captured the attention of all the guys at Waverly. And she hadn't even done it by being cute and bubbly and genuine, like Jenny Humphrey had. She'd done it by beating Tinsley at her own manipulative, backstabbing game. What had Tinsley done except expose Isla's past—which, if the reaction was anything to go by, was only going to make her more beloved and adored? Tinsley didn't think they were anything close to even.

But she also had no real interest in taking the game to another level. No wonder she felt so strange. Resignation wasn't a feeling she'd ever encountered before.

"I shouldn't have done that to you," Isla continued in a low voice. She didn't look at Tinsley as she washed her hands. "I kind of took the whole bad-girl thing too far. I just really wanted to start over, and I was trying way too hard."

Tinsley opened her mouth to say something suitably cutting but shrugged instead. "If it's any consolation, I never would have suspected," she said. "Your transformation is pretty stunning."

"Thanks," Isla said. She looked at Tinsley then, her expression wry. "I think."

"Sure." Tinsley flipped her hair back from her face. "I fully believed you were a devious, manipulative, scheming party girl, and had been since birth."

She didn't say *like me*. But Isla smiled anyway. "That's the nicest thing you could have said to me."

Tinsley laughed softly and then nodded toward the door, motioning for Isla to walk in front of her. *Keep your friends close and your enemies closer,* she thought, keeping an eye on Isla's back as they walked into the party. And maybe it wasn't beyond the realm of possibility that dork-turned-schemer Isla Dresden, Tinsley's biggest challenge yet, might be both.

"Ladies," Heath said as they emerged, stepping forward with a glass of punch in each hand, "I hope you didn't get into a cat-fight in there. And if you did, I certainly hope you filmed it."

Isla winked at Tinsley before gliding off toward a group of Owls from the jazz ensemble who were gazing at her in open adoration. *They* actually did erupt into spontaneous applause when she approached, but then, Isla's transformation was probably their communal wet dream.

"Cheers," Heath said, handing Tinsley a glass of punch and redirecting her attention to his wicked cheekbones and Armani-clad body. "Drink up. You look seriously sober."

"I thought I'd be on your shit list after my slideshow," Tinsley said, staring at the glass in her hand. "Is this drink spiked?"

"Of course the drink is spiked," Heath replied, his green eyes twinkling. "But why do you say that like it's a bad thing?" He clanked their glasses together. "And I thought that slideshow rocked. Who knew such hotness could come from such tragic origins? I might have to pay closer attention to the loser contingent around here. Who knows what's lurking under all that bad hair and all those baggy clothes?"

Tinsley considered him for a moment. "You thought it was funny?"

"Of course I thought it was funny. Please. She looked heinous," he said.

"But she's your precious little Isla," Tinsley said, her bitterness more apparent than she'd intended. "You *rushed* over to ask her if she still had her stupid costume!"

Heath gazed at Tinsley, his handsome face amused. "Imagine how hot that costume would be on her *now*," he said. "The tutu, particularly, especially if she wasn't wearing any—"

Tinsley rolled her eyes and started to turn away, but Heath reached over and touched her arm. She stopped and looked at him. The music was blaring, and a pack of drunken seniors had their arms flung around one another's shoulders as they sang along—but all Tinsley could see was Heath.

"Anyway," he said more quietly. His gaze was warm. "She's not *my* precious anything."

"Uh-huh." Tinsley took a careful sip of her drink, savoring the fruity punch and the kick of rum beneath, a Ferro specialty. "You've been slobbering all over her like a rabid dog."

"I slobber all over everyone," he said matter-of-factly with a shrug. "I don't like her or anything." He smiled. "But you thought I did, didn't you? Finally, after all these years, I got your attention."

Tinsley shook her head at him dismissively. But she was secretly more pleased than she wanted to admit. "How old are you?" she asked, pretending to scoff. "You were mean to me to get me to notice you? What's next, throwing sand at me in the sandbox? Stealing my crayons?"

"Give me a break, Tinsley," Heath retorted. He smirked. "Besides, it worked, didn't it?"

"Not at all," she lied. They both smiled. Tinsley tossed her hair back. "It just made me wonder what was wrong with you that you thought that wannabe was so captivating. After all," she said loftily, "I know who you lie awake at night and fantasize about." She moved closer and let their shoulders brush before drawing back. "You always have, and you always will."

Heath leaned in and traced a finger down Tinsley's bare arm. She shivered involuntarily. "We can take that out of the fantasy realm any time you like, babe. Just say the word."

"The word is *no,* you idiot," Tinsley said with a laugh.

But she didn't feel the need to walk away just yet, either.

A WAVERLY OWL FACES CONFLICT HEAD-ON, EVEN
WHEN SHE WANTS TO EAT A BOX OF CHOCOLATES
AND CRY.

Brett pushed through the heavy glass doors and out into
the cold night, leaving the noise of the dance behind
her. She didn't think she could possibly feel worse after
Sebastian had walked away, leaving her standing by herself.
Until she saw the way Jenny looked at her.

Jenny had taken off before Brett could do more than stare
at her, leaving Brett to try to piece together what had happened. Searching the crowd, she'd spotted Isaac with another
girl and instantly figured it out. Clearly, Isaac hadn't broken
things off with his girlfriend, and the whole thing must have
come crashing down pretty quickly. Jenny obviously blamed
Brett, and how could Brett even argue with that? Look what

she had done! So she did the only thing she could—she went after Jenny. She ran all the way across campus, trying to catch up with her.

Brett threw open the front doors of Dumbarton and ran inside, only a few steps behind.

"Wait!" she cried. Jenny obviously heard her. Her shoulders tensed. She didn't turn around, but she stopped a few feet in front of the common room.

"I'm so sorry," Brett began, hurrying to Jenny's side.

"How did you know?" Jenny refused to look at Brett. She stared straight ahead as if searching for answers on the common room walls. "Did he tell you?"

"No." Brett suddenly felt deeply ashamed of herself. What had she been thinking? She couldn't even remember how she'd justified looking at Isaac's texts. She couldn't justify any of her behavior lately. "I, um, saw a message on his phone."

Jenny turned to look at her then, hurt and confusion making her brown eyes seem bigger and brighter than usual. She gave Brett a questioning sort of look.

"I don't know. . . ." Brett said. She felt shaky. "I just . . . I never meant to lie to you, Jenny. I swear. He said that he was going to break it off with her and tell you the truth. He promised!"

"Yeah, well . . ." Jenny swallowed, fighting back tears. "It turns out that Isaac is actually a big liar, so . . ."

"I never meant for you to find out like this," Brett swore fervently. "I really thought he would tell you. I mean, he knew I knew. I don't know what he thought was going to happen.

I certainly didn't think something like this . . ." Her voice trailed away.

Jenny let out a sound that was somewhere between a sigh and a sob and walked into the common room. Brett followed. Jenny sat down on one of the cozy navy blue couches and hugged herself.

"Her name is Molly," she said. She looked at the thick carpet beneath her feet. Her voice was thick with misery. "She seemed nice. He told her he was sick. She's really mad at him, too. He lied to her."

"Jenny . . ." Brett wanted to reach over and hug her, but Jenny's arms were crossed, and Brett wasn't sure how she would react. Maybe she didn't consider Brett a friend anymore. The very thought made Brett's stomach ache. But there was nothing to do but sit there, and wait.

"I'm not mad at you," Jenny said after a moment. She sighed. "I mean, not really. This isn't your fault." She hugged herself tighter. "I guess I should know by now that if I like someone, that pretty much means I should stay away from him, because he's destined to just . . . lie. About everything." She thought of Julian's sweet smile. He was a great guy, but he'd lied to her, too, hadn't he? Just like everyone else.

"I'm so, so sorry," Brett whispered. "I know I should have told you. I just . . ."

"It doesn't matter," Jenny said. "I forgive you." She rolled her eyes. "I mean, what would I have done if you'd told me? I would have asked him about it and he probably would've lied. So maybe this was going to happen no matter what."

But Brett knew that it *did* matter. It was like the hard, tight knot she'd been carrying around inside her had finally come undone, and she could see the truth. And the truth wasn't very pretty.

"It's like I've gone completely insane," she said slowly. "I don't even know who I am anymore. I've turned into this paranoid, jealous, crazy person." She shook her head, tucking her bob behind her ears. "It's like all I could think about was Isla Dresden and how she was flirting with Sebastian."

"What?" Jenny frowned at her. "Sebastian would never—"

"I know," Brett said miserably, "but it's pretty much beside the point now. I've messed everything up with him. I mean, would you want to be with a lunatic?"

Jenny shrugged her shoulders and smiled at her friend. "I think you're being kind of hard on yourself," she said in a soft voice. "Love makes you do crazy things."

Brett stared at her for a moment. It was so . . . obvious. It was one more thing she'd completely failed to notice. One more glaring truth. It seemed to light up the common room, bouncing off the polished wood and elegant couches and collecting in the middle of the Oriental rug in the center, like heat.

"Jenny," she said thickly, "thank you. Really. And . . . I really am sorry about Isaac."

"Me too," Jenny said, making a face. "Jerk."

"But . . ." Brett made a helpless gesture. "I really have to find Sebastian."

Jenny should have hated her for that, Brett thought. And maybe she would—

But instead, her friend just smiled.

"Go," she said.

Brett pounded on the door to his room. Sebastian took a long time to open it, and when he did, he looked cranky. He had changed out of his sleek suit and was in sweats and a beat-up T-shirt. But he was still the best-looking guy Brett had ever laid eyes on.

"I don't want to talk about this anymore," Sebastian said, his voice curt. He stood in the doorway, his dark eyes brooding and challenging when they met hers. Just like they always were. Brett was breathless, her knees weak beneath her. "Seriously. I'm already in a shitty mood and—"

"I'm sorry," Brett said simply.

His dark brows rose. "Oh yeah?"

"Yeah." She shrugged. "Everything you said is true. I've been acting completely insane."

"I know," he said, but his voice was just a little bit softer.

"But I finally realized why," she said. This was the scary part. She'd never said this before, and she wasn't entirely sure she could say it now. Panic skittered along her nerves, but she took a deep breath. "It's because I . . . I love you."

It felt as if entire years passed while she watched Sebastian's face. The words were out there now, and she couldn't take them back. What if he laughed? What if he said something mean? What if he didn't love her?

But then, finally, when she thought she might burst into tears, he smiled.

"Wow," he said, his dark eyes warm as he gazed at her.

"Yeah," she said, her voice shaking.

"Apology accepted," Sebastian murmured. He closed the distance between them and pulled Brett into his arms. "I love you, too, idiot."

And then he kissed her.

A WAVERLY OWL KNOWS THE VALUE OF A SECOND CHANCE.

Brandon wasn't sure why he'd stayed to watch the stupid slideshow. It was the same every year. The same people in the same poses, and, if he were honest about it, he really didn't need to see a picture of himself with Callie. Not after tonight's revelations. It was more than past time to go home and lick his wounds.

Yes, Heath, he thought darkly as he walked past the dance floor and spotted his roommate dancing way too close to Tinsley Carmichael, who should have known better, *I'm going to pull the shades and listen to Kelly Clarkson, and you're just going to have to deal with it.*

"Hey, Brandon."

He turned to see Cora standing before him. She looked cute tonight, in a little black dress that showed off her surprisingly long legs, her auburn hair up in a complicated sort of twist. It wasn't an Isla-worthy transformation or anything, but without her glasses taking over her whole face, his Perfect Match had really pretty eyes. Brown, but shot through with gold.

"I saw what happened," she began.

Of course she had. *Everyone* had. It would have been humiliating, if Brandon still had it in him to care.

"Listen," he said, before she could say anything else, "I know we're supposed to hang out tonight, but I really just want to get out of here. I'm sorry. It's, um, been a long night." Around them, people were dancing in packs and singing along to the music at ear-shattering volume. It was far too much mayhem. Brandon didn't want to watch Benny Cunningham and Sage Francis dirty dance with Lon Baruzza, he wanted to sit in his dark, quiet room and just think. And, yeah, maybe listen to some angsty pop music.

"No, of course," Cora said. "I just . . . there's just something I need to tell you."

He sighed and attempted to smile.

"Okay," he said. He tried to sound interested. After all, she was a perfectly nice girl. She'd tried to help with Callie, and she hardly even knew him. That had to count for something.

She wrung her hands together. "So," she said, sounding anxious, "the thing is, I run the Waverly Computer Society. You probably didn't know that."

"Um, no," Brandon said. He realized that he hadn't attempted to find out anything about Cora, despite the fact that they'd been matched. He felt a little bad about that. He'd just been so wrapped up in his Callie drama—which he'd dumped on Cora. "But that's, uh, really cool."

"I'm the one who's in charge of Perfect Match," she said. "I kind of inherited it." Brandon watched, fascinated, as her entire face turned bright red. "And I, um. I've had a crush on you since you were a freshman." She coughed slightly. "Pairing us up was the only way I could think of to talk to you."

Brandon felt himself smile. Despite the weirdness of it all, how could anyone not be a little bit flattered by that? Someone had liked him from afar. And had gone completely out of her way just to meet him. Okay, maybe it was a little bit creepy. But in a nice way.

"Really?" he asked, touched. He considered her for a moment. "Does that happen a lot?"

"No!" She looked appalled. "I would *never* tamper with the matches! We actually take that very seriously . . ." Her voice trailed away and she looked sheepish. "It was just . . . it was only you. I'm really sorry. I hope you'll forgive me."

"You're forgiven," Brandon assured her. Who was he to judge people with hopeless crushes? He kind of liked the idea that there was someone out there pining for him the way he'd pined for Callie all this time.

"Thank you." She was still blushing.

"Wait a minute," Brandon said as a new thought occurred to him. "So if you, uh, like me, why'd you help me try to get Callie back?"

Cora turned even redder, which Brandon would have

thought was physically impossible. "There's one other thing," she said miserably. "When I first ran the matches, you were actually paired up with Callie. How could I *not* help you? You were supposed to be with her. You *are* supposed to be with her."

Brandon looked at her for a moment, surprised at how empty he felt when he thought about Callie. Suddenly he wished he hadn't wasted so much time on a girl he didn't know the way he'd thought he did. A girl who did sneaky things without even blinking. A girl who could hurt him as much and as often as she had. Except—was that even her fault? Brandon had pretty much thrown himself on the ground and begged her to kick him, hadn't he?

"I only got Callie because I deliberately answered all the questions the way I thought she would," he heard himself confessing to Cora. It was funny—this was the second time he'd opened up to her like this, without even really meaning to. It was something about the way she looked at him, maybe. Like she believed in him.

"I'm pathetic," he said, almost laughing, because it was almost funny. He felt better the minute it was out there. The minute he admitted it. "That's painfully obvious."

"No," Cora said, smiling sweetly. "Not pathetic. Dedicated, maybe."

"Anyway," Brandon said, "Callie and I are *not* supposed to be together."

Cora's bright red embarrassment had faded, and as Brandon spoke, she started to get a hopeful glint in her brown eyes.

And suddenly Brandon couldn't think of any reason why he shouldn't kiss the girl who liked him—rather than chase after the one who didn't. It was Valentine's Day. What could be more romantic? He leaned forward and pressed his lips to hers.

And to his surprise, he really, really liked it.

A WAVERLY OWL KNOWS THAT SOMETIMES THE DESTINATION MATTERS MORE THAN THE JOURNEY.

Callie sat on her bed in the dark.

She hadn't bothered to change her clothes. She hadn't even cried. It seemed like a luxury she didn't deserve. She just sat, slumped over on her silk-quilted bedspread, her mind spinning like a top as she tried to figure out how everything could have gone so horribly wrong.

It was her fault. She knew that. She'd lost both Easy and Brandon tonight, and she wasn't stupid enough to try to talk herself into believing otherwise. She'd seen the way they'd both looked at her—worse, she'd *felt* it.

They hated her. Which they had every right to do.

So of course it was only now that she'd lost both of them, thanks to her ridiculous stoner plan, that she recognized a truth she should have known all along: she'd wanted Easy to win. She'd wanted him to fight the hardest. Once she'd heard that

Easy was collecting hearts for her, she hadn't even *thought* about what Brandon was doing.

Everything seemed so obvious to her now, sitting in the dark. But somehow, she'd gotten it all confused. Being with Brandon had seemed like the better, safer, nobler choice. And yet the truth was that it had always been Easy for her. Always. No matter how she messed it up, or got freaked out, or even what he did to ruin things when it was his turn.

She heard the clatter of stones against her window, but she didn't move. He couldn't really be there. Not after everything that had happened . . .

Callie closed her eyes and hoped.

And when the next pebble hit the window, she jumped to her feet and headed for the door. She took the stairs two at a time, breathing too heavily, desperate to get outside.

When she pushed through the door, the February night was bitterly cold, but Callie barely noticed. Because Easy stood there, waiting for her.

They looked at each other for a long moment. Easy's dark blue eyes seemed to see right through her and made Callie want to cry the tears she'd held back before. Not because she'd lost him, but because she could still love him so much when she thought she'd never have the chance to be with him again.

He didn't speak. He shrugged out of his jacket and stepped closer so he could drape it around her shoulders. Callie murmured a thank-you and pulled the jacket closer over her bare arms. It smelled like Easy. Cigarettes and soap and the faint hint of hay.

"Easy," she whispered.

"I know you must have been confused," he said. He was still standing close, his long, rangy body emanating heat. Callie wanted to bury her head in his chest and feel his arms around her, almost more than she wanted to keep breathing. "I came back so suddenly, and you were with Brandon. I get that you must have freaked out a little bit."

"I didn't know what to do," she admitted, but then she bit her lip. "But Easy, that's the thing. I don't know why I was so confused. . . ."

"You were trying to move on," he said quietly. "Kind of like me in the beginning of the year, I guess. I don't know why we keep doing that."

Callie didn't really want to talk about those confusing weeks right after school started, when Easy had broken up with her to be with Jenny. But maybe Easy was right. Maybe it was the same thing she'd been doing with Brandon. Things with Brandon were always so predictable, so calm. Everything with Easy, on the other hand, was complicated. Everything.

But that didn't mean it wasn't right.

Easy's eyes glowed. "I wish you'd talked to me about stuff before you just broke up with me," he said. "But I'm sorry I messed things up tonight. I really did want to dance with you."

"Easy . . ." She could hear the tears in her voice, taste them in the back of her throat.

"I guess we'll never know who found the most hearts on campus," he said. He reached over and fished around in the pocket of the jacket she was wearing like a cape. He pulled out one lone red heart and held it in his hand. "But I brought you this."

Callie felt her tears spill over then, and she didn't even bother to wipe them away or try to save her mascara. She just let them fall. She reached over and covered his palm—and the heart—with her hand.

"I only need one," she told him, losing herself in the way he looked at her, in the sure knowledge that, this time, Easy was really giving her his heart. And she was giving him hers.

For good.

EPILOGUE

Bright May sunshine poured through the open windows of Dumbarton, lighting up the room and carrying with it the sweet smell of new spring flowers and the briny kick of the Hudson River. Music poured from almost every window and open door in the dorm, as Owls packed up their belongings and got ready for their summer destinations. The long hallways echoed with competing iPods, pounding feet, and the squeals and laughter of the girls as they said their good-byes.

Jenny sat back on her heels and looked at the stack of boxes in front of her. "I don't think we have enough packing tape," she said, not for the first time. Across the room, Callie dumped her last armload of clothes into her final box and scrunched up her face as she peered into it.

"We'll be fine," she said dubiously. She squatted down and started shoving the pile of clothes down, trying to force them all to fit. "When are you leaving for Prague?"

"The day after tomorrow," Jenny said. She used the last of the packing tape and stood up. "I haven't seen my mom in a while, so it should be cool."

"Plus it's *Prague*," Callie said with a smile. "Which is much more exciting than Georgia." She finished jamming her clothes into the box and started wrestling with the cardboard flaps, pushing one beneath the next to make them hold without tape. "I'm already bored out of my mind just thinking about it. Summer in Buckhead is like living in someone's sweaty armpit, I'm not even kidding."

"That sounds great," Jenny said sarcastically. She wrinkled her nose. "But the last time I checked, Georgia was pretty close to Kentucky. . . ."

"Yes," Callie said with a giggle. "There is that." She climbed to her feet and smiled at Jenny. "Easy and I will definitely be seeing a lot of each other this summer. His dad already loves me, and my mother likes it when I have things to do that don't end up in the papers, so I'm thinking it might just be an okay summer after all."

There was a softness about her that hadn't been there before, Jenny thought. Callie and Easy had gotten back together on Valentine's Day and had *stayed* together for the rest of the term, happier than they'd ever been before. Maybe love really could conquer all.

She took a final look around Dumbarton 303, making sure they weren't leaving anything behind. With their posters off the walls and their belongings packed into boxes, the room seemed smaller. Nothing more than bare white walls, a dark wood floor, three empty cots, and dust. The memories were hers to take with her.

"What are you guys doing?" Tinsley's unmistakable voice came from the doorway. "I texted both of you at least seventeen times."

She stood with a couple of small boxes in her arms and a bag slung over her shoulder. Next to her was Brett, who was laden down with a huge pile of her belongings. Tinsley had a smudge of dust on her forehead from packing up her things, yet she still managed to look elegant.

"Want to take a load down?" Brett asked, her voice muffled behind a box. Her red hair reached her shoulders, no longer ruthlessly maintained in her old bob. She'd stopped dyeing it fire-engine red, and it was now a beautiful, natural russet color.

Jenny hoisted her own duffel bag to her shoulder and took a last look at the boxes that housekeeping services would ship out before the end of the week.

Callie smirked at Tinsley. "You look like a Sherpa," she said. "All I'm bringing is my carry-on."

"Bitch," Tinsley replied, smiling, while Callie grabbed her giant hobo bag and the satchel she used as a carry-on.

"But I'll walk down to the parking lot with you all," Callie continued. "For moral support."

Jenny kept pace with Brett as they headed down the stairs and out the propped-open side door into the quad. The grass was green and lush. A few Owls who had finished packing were picnicking, sitting in little groups in the sunshine. Alison

Quentin was blaring some kind of guitar solo from her bedroom window up above the doorway. She yelled a good-bye out the window, and Callie waved enthusiastically in response.

"I'm so jealous that you and Sebastian are road-tripping," Jenny said, grinning at Brett. "I've always wanted to do that."

"You say that," Brett replied with a giggle, "but you don't realize that Seb is *very serious* about his car. It requires a lot of maintenance. And, you know, we're from New Jersey. The road trip is like an art."

"A summerlong art!" Jenny said with a laugh. "That's pretty impressive."

"We're going to camp the whole way, hit the Dakotas and Montana and Idaho," Brett said dreamily. "Spend some time in Seattle and drive down the coast to California. Then take our time coming back. The Grand Canyon. Austin. New Orleans."

"That sounds amazing," Jenny said, sighing happily over the sounds of laughter from Callie and Tinsley behind them.

"We just have to get Seb to Rutgers in August," Brett said. "Everything else is up to us."

"You'd better send a million pictures," Callie said from behind them. "All of you. Maybe there should be a daily photo assignment."

"That sounds a lot like homework," Tinsley complained. "No, thank you."

"An assignment to make *my* summer more fun!" Callie protested. "What could be better than that?"

"How about no assignments at all?" Tinsley retorted, but there was laughter in her voice.

They walked across the quad in the spring sunshine, headed for the parking lot. Benny Cunningham and Sage Francis were walking arm in arm toward Dumbarton, and they all chorused their *goodbye*s and *text me*s when they passed on the pathway. Celine Colista and Verena Arvenal were lying out on a blanket, soaking up rays and gossiping rather than packing up their rooms. Brandon Buchanan and his girlfriend, Cora, sat together on one of the stone benches, their heads close together while they talked intently. He and Cora seemed to really be into each other—Jenny had heard him telling an incredulous Heath Ferro the other night that he and Cora were definitely planning to stay together even after she headed to MIT in the fall.

A group of guys were playing Frisbee in the farther part of the quad, nearer to Richards. Teague Williams and Ryan Reynolds went down in a tackle that had them both laughing. Alan St. Girard was sauntering along behind, looking as half-asleep as ever. Heath Ferro grabbed the Frisbee out of a sweet throw by Lon Baruzza and then threw it back. It curved through the air, orange and blue, headed straight for Lon's head.

"Hey!" Heath yelled, loud enough to get even Benny's and Sage's attention, way in the other direction. His shirt was off and his tanned chest glistened in the sunshine. He was still smarmy Heath Ferro, but he was also undeniably gorgeous. From a safe distance. "Carmichael! You'd better not be taking that hot ass off campus without letting me say goodbye to it!"

Tinsley smirked, but Jenny could tell she was pleased.

"Excuse me," Tinsley said, heaving a long-suffering sigh. "I have to go deal with that mess." She adjusted her bag on her shoulder and made a face at Callie, who rolled her eyes—but then relented and smiled when Tinsley hugged her.

Tinsley gave Brett and Jenny hugs as well and then sauntered toward Heath, her heels digging into the soft earth as she headed across the grass. It was funny that they'd been put together for Perfect Match back in February, Jenny thought, because they really were each other's perfect match. Their flirtation had continued since Valentine's Day, but Jenny doubted that they'd ever really be a couple. They were both too pretty and too dangerous. It would be like an explosion waiting to happen.

As they neared the parking lot, Brett picked up the pace when she saw Sebastian waiting by his beloved Mustang.

"How can you possibly have more stuff?" he groaned, but he was smiling as he took the boxes out of Brett's arms, kissing her on the nose as he did so.

"We're dropping all of this off at home," Brett reminded Sebastian. "You can pack the car for the road trip any way you want."

Callie gave her a long hug, then Jenny stepped forward and did the same. She could hardly remember a time when she hadn't known Brett—and she was sad that she wouldn't see her every day this summer. It seemed like a dream to Jenny now, that there had ever been a *before* Waverly.

Sebastian gunned his powerful motor, and then the two girls waved, watching as the black car peeled out of the parking lot toward Waverly's majestic iron gates.

"I guess it's just us," Callie said, turning to Jenny and resting her hands on her hips.

Easy jogged down the path from Richards. Callie turned and smiled at him as he drew closer. Jenny did, too, genuinely glad to see him. The ache that she used to feel when she saw him had disappeared completely. Maybe she'd accepted what it seemed like Callie and Easy had finally accepted—they were made for each other.

"The car the governor sent is here," he said as he approached. He nodded a hello to Jenny. "The driver is worried about traffic getting out to JFK."

"And by the driver," Callie drawled, "he really means my mother, who's probably calling the poor driver every fifteen seconds to stress him out."

"You do have a habit of missing flights, Cal," Easy said. His smile when he looked at her was so sweet and intimate, Jenny had to turn away.

"Off to Atlanta we go," Callie said with a sigh. "I'm going to have to think up something to do, or the boredom really might kill me." But she reached for Easy while she spoke and took his hand. Jenny had a feeling they weren't going to be bored on the trip at all.

"Keep me posted, whatever you do," Jenny said. The three of them hugged their good-byes before Easy led Callie away.

"I thought you were coming to Kentucky and learning how to be a serious horseback rider, Cal," he teased her as they walked away. "Didn't you tell me that?"

"In your dreams, maybe," Callie replied, laughing.

Jenny was all alone. She let out a breath and shifted her duffel bag to the ground. At various spots along the edge of the asphalt, there were other Owls with boxes and bags, either loading their stuff into idling cars or, like Jenny, waiting to be picked up. She told herself she wasn't feeling lonely, exactly. She just wasn't used to a whole lot of solitary time anymore. She was used to a shared life now. Callie, Tinsley, Brett, and Jenny had been inseparable this past semester. It was going to take some getting used to, being just one-fourth of their foursome.

Rufus had called to say he was on his way and had checked in several times since then, so Jenny expected him at any moment. She wished he'd come sooner. She laughed a little to herself, remembering how insistent she'd been about taking the train to Waverly at the beginning of the year. She'd been too embarrassed to have anyone meet her dad—the thought of it had practically killed her. Now she wished her friends could have waited a little longer, to meet Rufus and see her off.

She sat down on the curb and pulled out her sketchbook. Ever since she'd gotten an A on her Jan Plan project, prompting the dean to rethink his policy on underclassmen not being allowed to work alone, she'd been feeling confident about her work, and inspired. Jenny's fingers flew across the page as she started to draw whatever came to her mind: The spire on the top of the Waverly chapel. The big bay windows in Dumbarton 303. Callie's head thrown back in a ridiculous belly laugh. Tinsley and Brett whispering to each other. Her own face in the mirror of Dumbarton 303. All the funny, touching, and tumultuous moments that had made up her year at Waverly—maybe the best year of her life.

She looked up, and there was her dad driving up in her brother Dan's beat-up old Buick Skylark. Jenny had to smile at the difference between the Humphrey family vehicle and all the Mercedeses, Lexus SUVs, and limos that littered the rest of the parking area. And then she *really* had to smile, thinking about how humiliated she would have been by this back in the fall. She would have been mortified. But over the course of the year, something had happened to make her less embarrassed. Maybe, just maybe, she'd grown up—if only a little.

Rufus climbed out of the car to give Jenny a hug. "My favorite daughter!" he cried.

"Very funny, Dad," Jenny said, but she hugged him tight.

They set about loading her things into the car. But when she went to pick up her heavy duffel bag, a tall, lanky figure appeared in front of her.

"Let me get that for you."

Jenny looked up at Julian. He was so tall—ridiculously tall, especially next to a midget like her—and he was so cute. His smile was sweet and his golden brown eyes glowed like summer. She couldn't help but smile at him.

"Juniors shouldn't have to carry their own things." He grinned. "That's what we measly underclassmen are for."

"You're not a freshman anymore," she pointed out. "They'll have to stop torturing you."

Julian swung the duffel into the backseat of the Buick and then turned to grin down at Jenny. "I can dish out a little torture myself now," he said. "It could be fun."

"Sure," she said. "But I can't exactly picture you being mean to anyone."

Julian shrugged, but he was still grinning. "Did I hear you're going to Prague?"

"My mom lives there," Jenny explained. She hadn't really thought about her summer, but when she'd realized that everyone was scattering and she'd be on her own, she'd decided to go to Europe. The year before, at this time, she never would have considered living across the world for an entire summer, but she was no longer the Jenny who was afraid to take risks.

She looked up at Julian, and as the sun came out from behind a cloud, it danced on his messy hair and defined cheekbones. She wanted to draw him so badly, her hands itched.

"You're lucky." Julian shoved his hands in his pockets. "I'll be in Seattle, hanging out with my parents. Not quite as much fun as exploring Prague, I assure you." He smiled at her. "Will you keep in touch?"

"I will," Jenny said, and the words hung there between them, like a promise.

He stepped forward and pulled her into a hug, and a tingling sensation rushed through her, the way it always did when she got too close to Julian McCafferty.

"I'll see you," he said as she opened the passenger door.

Jenny just smiled. Definitely.

She buckled herself into her seat. As her dad pulled out onto the main campus drive, she looked back at Waverly's stately, graceful buildings. The red bricks and New England white clapboard all blended together with the lush green lawns, the flowering trees, and the tall birch trees.

It had been a great year, she thought with a smile, settling back into her seat. But she had a feeling that next year was going to be even better.

Spotted:
Blair, Serena, and Nate, Home for the Holidays.

*Four years, four winter breaks.
A lot can change…but some things never do.*

i will always love you
a gossip girl
novel

In paperback October 2010.

Welcome to Poppy.

A poppy is a beautiful blooming red flower
(like the one on the spine of this book). It is also
the name of the home of your favorite books.

Poppy takes the real world and makes it
a little funnier, a little more fabulous.

Poppy novels are wild, witty, and inspiring.
They were written just for you.

So sit back, get comfy, and pick a Poppy.

poppy

www.pickapoppy.com